AS RED AS BLOOD

AS RED AS BLOOD

BOOK 1 IN THE AS RED AS BLOOD TRILOGY

SALLA SIMUKKA

Translated from the Finnish
by Owen F. Witesman

CROWN
NEW YORK

Text copyright © 2013 Salla Simukka

Translation copyright © 2014 Owen F. Witesman

All rights reserved. Published in the United States by Crown Books for Young Readers, an imprint of Random House Children's Books, a division of Penguin Random House LLC, New York. Originally published in trade paperback by Skyscape, New York, in 2014.

Crown and the colophon are registered trademarks of Penguin Random House LLC.

Visit us on the Web! randomhouseteens.com

Educators and librarians, for a variety of teaching tools, visit us at RHTeachersLibrarians.com

Library of Congress Cataloging-in-Publication Data is available upon request.

ISBN 978-1-5247-1341-6 (trade) — ISBN 978-1-5247-1342-3 (lib. bdg.) — ISBN 978-1-5247-1343-0 (ebook)

Printed in the United States of America

10 9 8 7 6 5 4 3 2 1

First Edition

Random House Children's Books supports the First Amendment and celebrates the right to read.

AS RED AS BLOOD

Once upon a time in midwinter, as flakes of snow fell like feathers from heaven, a queen sat sewing at her window, which was framed in black ebony wood.

As she sewed, gazing out at the snow, the needle pricked her finger, bringing forth three drops of blood, which fell onto the snow. Seeing the beauty of the red upon the white, she thought within herself, "Would that I had a child as white as snow, as red as blood, and as black as the wood in this window frame."

SUNDAY, FEBRUARY 28

1

GLITTERING WHITE LAY ALL AROUND. OVER THE OLD SNOW, A new, clean layer of soft flakes had fallen fifteen minutes earlier. Fifteen minutes earlier, everything had still been possible. The world had looked beautiful, the future flickering somewhere in the distance: brighter, freer, more peaceful. A future worth risking everything, worth going all-in, worth trying to make a break for it.

Fifteen minutes earlier, a light, downy snowfall had spread a thin feather blanket over the old snow. Then it had ceased, as suddenly as it had begun, followed by rays of sunshine breaking through the clouds. Hardly any days all winter had been this beautiful.

Now each moment saw more red encroaching on the white, spreading, gaining ground, creeping forward through the crystals, staining them as it went. Some of the red had flown farther, a shrieking, bright crimson spattering the snow.

Natalia Smirnova stared with brown eyes at the red-flecked snow, seeing nothing. Thinking nothing. Hoping nothing. Fearing nothing.

Ten minutes earlier, Natalia had hoped and feared more than ever before in her life. With trembling hands, she had stuffed money into her authentic Louis Vuitton handbag, anxiously listening for even the tiniest rustling from outside. She had tried to steady her nerves, assuring herself that everything was fine. She had a plan. But at the same time, she had known that no plan was ever perfect. An intricate edifice carefully constructed over months can collapse at the barest nudge.

The purse had also contained a passport and plane ticket to Moscow. She wasn't taking anything else. At the Moscow airport, her brother would be waiting with a rental car, ready to drive her hundreds of miles to a *dacha* only a few people knew about. There, her mother would be waiting with three-year-old Olga, the daughter she hadn't seen in more than a year. Would her little girl even remember her? But no matter. A month or two hiding out in the countryside would give them time to get to know each other again. While they waited until she believed they were safe. While they waited for the world to forget about Natalia Smirnova.

Natalia had stifled the nagging voice in her head that insisted no one would forget her at all. That they wouldn't allow her to disappear. She had assured herself that she wasn't so important that they couldn't simply find someone to replace her if need be. And going to the effort of tracking her down would be too much bother anyway.

In this line of work, people disappeared now and then, usually taking some money along with them. That was just one of the risks of doing business—an unavoidable loss like the spoiled fruit a grocery store had to throw out.

Natalia hadn't counted the money. She'd simply stuffed as much of it as she could into her bag. Some of the bills had gotten crumpled, but that didn't matter. A crumpled five-hundred-euro bill was worth just as much as a crisp one. You could still buy three months of food with it, maybe four if you were really careful. You could still use it to buy a person's silence for long enough. For lots of people, five hundred euros was the price of a secret.

Natalia Smirnova, age twenty, lay facedown, her cheek in the cold snow. Not feeling the prickling of the ice against her skin. Not feeling the frigid chill of thirteen below on her bare earlobes.

The man had sung about a woman named Natalia to her in a gruff voice, off-key. Natalia hadn't liked the song. The Natalia in it was from Ukraine, but she was from Russia. On the other hand, she had liked the man who sang and stroked her hair. She'd just tried not to listen to the words. Fortunately, that had been easy. She'd known some Finnish, understanding much more than she could speak, but when she stopped trying and let her mind relax, the foreign words ran together, losing their meaning and becoming nothing more than combinations of sounds falling out of the man's mouth as he hummed sweetly against Natalia's neck.

Five minutes earlier, Natalia had been thinking about that man and his slightly clumsy hands. Would he miss her? Maybe a bit. Maybe just a little bit. But not enough, because he had never loved her, not really. If he had loved her, really loved her, he would have solved Natalia's problems for her, as he'd promised to do so many times. Now Natalia had to solve her problems for herself.

Two minutes earlier, Natalia had snapped her handbag shut, which bulged with cash. Quickly, she'd tidied up and then glanced at herself in the front hall mirror. Bleached blond hair, brown eyes, thin eyebrows, and shining red lips. She had been pale, with dark circles under her eyes from staying up too late. She had just been leaving. In her mouth, she had tasted freedom and fear, both of which had a metallic tang.

Two minutes earlier, she had looked her reflection in the eye and raised her chin. This was her chance to make a break, and she was taking it.

That's when Natalia heard the key turning in the lock. She had frozen in place, straining her ears. One set of footsteps, then another, and a third. The Troika. The Troika were coming through the door.

All she could do was run.

One minute earlier, Natalia had charged through the kitchen toward the patio door. She'd fumbled with the lock. Her hands had been shaking too much to get the door unlatched. Then, by some miracle, it had given way, and Natalia had run across the snow-covered terrace into the garden. Her leather boots had sunk in the fresh snow, but she'd pressed on without looking back. She hadn't heard anything. She had thought for a moment that she might make it after all, that she might escape, that she might actually win.

Thirty seconds earlier, a pistol fitted with a silencer had fired with a dull snap, and a bullet had pierced the back of Natalia Smirnova's coat and skin, barely missing her spine and ripping through her internal organs and, finally, the handle of her Louis Vuitton bag, which she had been clutching to her chest. She had fallen forward into the pure, untouched snow.

The red puddle under Natalia continued to spread, consuming the snow all around. The red was still voracious and warm, but it cooled with each second that passed. One set of slow, heavy footfalls approached Natalia Smirnova as she lay in the snow. But she did not hear.

MONDAY, FEBRUARY 29, EARLY MORNING

2

THREE PEOPLE JOSTLED AT A SET OF BIG DOUBLE DOORS, EACH
wanting to be first inside.

"Yo, gimme a little space so I can get this key into the
hole."

"You can never get anything in the hole." Laughter, shush-
ing, more laughter.

"Hold on. That's it. Got it. And now turn it slow. Really
slow. Wow. This is amazing. I mean, can you believe how you
can unlock a door just by turning a key? How did anyone
ever come up with a system like this? If you ask me, this is the
thirteenth wonder of the world."

"Shut up and open the door."

Pushing the door wide, the three shoved each other as
they piled inside. One almost tripped. Another started making little high-pitched squeals and then laughed at how they
echoed in the big empty space. The third scratched his head

and then punched in the code for the building alarm, one digit at a time.

"One . . . seven . . . three . . . two. Hell yeah, I got it! And this is the fourteenth wonder of the world. That you can turn off an alarm by punching in some numbers. Hell yeah. Now I know what I'm gonna be when I grow up. I'm gonna be a locksmith. That's a job, right? Doing stuff with locks, I mean? Or maybe I'll be a security guard."

The other two weren't listening; they were already running along the building's long, empty hallways in the dark, shouting and giggling. The third took off after them. Laughter ricocheted off the walls, reverberating up the flights of stairs.

"We are the champions!"

Ampions. Mpions. Pions. Ions. Ons. Ns. S.

"And super fucking rich!"

Colliding on purpose, they fell to the floor, rolling around and snickering. Making angels on the wide tile floor. Then one of them remembered.

"We're rich, but the money is dirty."

"Yeah. Dirty money money money."

"Yo, we were supposed to go to the darkroom. That's why we came."

If they could only remember what had happened. Their memories were like a mist with glimpses of individual events flashing into view at random intervals. Someone vomiting. Some others skinny-dipping in a pool. A locked door that shouldn't have been locked. A broken crystal vase and shards that had cut someone's foot. Blood. Music throbbing too loudly. "Oops! . . . I Did It Again." A dead and buried single someone had put on repeat, who knows why. Someone crying inconsolably, sobbing that she didn't want help. The floor slick with spilled rum that smelled simultaneously sharp and sweet.

The memories refused to fit in any logical order. Who had brought the plastic bag? When had he brought it? Who had opened it, put their hand in, jerked it back out, and licked their finger? When had they realized?

Have to take something. Fast. Now.

"You guys got anything left? I could use another hit."

"I got these."

Three pills. One for each. Together, they placed them on their tongues and let them dissolve.

"That's got kick. Oh yeah. Nice kick."

In the darkroom. Darkness. Then one of them flipped the switch.

"Let there be light. And there was light."

Plastic bag onto the table. Bag open.

"Oh my God, that stinks."

"The money ain't the thing that stinks. Money never stinks."

"That's a shitload of cash."

"And we're splitting it fifty-fifty, three ways."

"This is so sick! Nothing like this has ever happened to me. I love you guys. I love the whole goddamn world."

"No kissing. I'll get all horny and lose my concentration."

"We could hump right here on the floor."

"No humping either. Now's time for some cleaning."

Processing trays. Water. Cash.

Then all they had to do was hang each bill up to dry.

"Now this is what I call money laundering."

MONDAY, FEBRUARY 29

3

"Up and at 'em! Come on, get your butt moving, sleepy-head. Don't even think about rolling over!"

Shouting filled Lumikki Andersson's ears. Unfortunately, the annoying voice was all too familiar since it was her own. She had recorded herself on her phone as an alarm because she thought that would get her out of a warm bed better than anything else. And it totally worked. Rolling over didn't even cross her mind.

Sitting bleary-eyed on the edge of the bed, she glanced at the Moomin cartoon calendar hanging on the wall. Monday, February 29. Leap day. The most pointless day in the world. Why couldn't it be an international holiday? It was just a left-over day, so why should anybody have to do anything useful or productive on it?

Lumikki shoved her feet into furry blue slippers and trudged to her kitchenette. Measuring out water and coffee, she put the moka pot on the stove to percolate. This morning, there was no way she could manage joining the land of the living without a strong cup of coffee. Outside it was still dark, far too dark to be awake. Without any light to reflect, even the tall snowdrifts didn't help. And the gloom wasn't going to let up for ages, holding all of Finland in its suffocating grip far into March.

She despised this part of the winter. Snow and cold. Too much of both. Spring wasn't just around the corner. Winter went on and on without any hope of ending, slowing down the world while it froze out of sheer boredom. She was cold at home. She was cold outside. She was cold at school. Strangely enough, sometimes she felt like the only time she wasn't cold was when she went swimming in the frosty hole they kept open in the ice down at the lake, but she couldn't spend all her time there. Pulling on a big gray wool sweater, Lumikki poured herself a cup of coffee. Then she went back into the only real room in her studio apartment, a princely hundred and eighty-two square feet, and curled up in a beat-up armchair to try to warm up. A draft came from the window even though she had added extra weather stripping in the fall.

The coffee tasted like coffee. But she didn't expect anything more from it. She couldn't stand all those strange, sugary chocolate hazelnut cardamom vanilla coffees. Coffee black and strong, facts straight up, and an apartment made for living in. That was how Lumikki liked to live her life.

Her mom was shocked the last time she visited. "Don't you want to decorate a little? Make it look like a home?"

No, she didn't. Lumikki had been living in her apartment for about a year and a half. Just a thick mattress on the floor, a desk, a laptop, and a comfy old chair. For the first few months, her mom kept insisting that she was going to buy a bed frame and a bookcase, but Lumikki had tenaciously refused. Her books sat in piles on the floor. The only "decorative element" was the black-and-white Moomin calendar. Why would she even bother nesting? This wasn't reality TV. She was just living here while she finished high school. The studio apartment wasn't home in the sense that she was going to put down roots for any longer than she had to. Once high school was done, Lumikki would be free to go wherever she wanted without having to miss anyone or anything.

Home wasn't seventy miles south in Riihimäki with her parents either. These days, she felt like a stranger there. The furniture and decorations reminded her of things she'd rather forget. Things she remembered more than enough in her dreams and nightmares.

Her parents' reaction to her moving away from home had been full of contradictions. Sometimes it seemed like it was a relief for them. It was true that the mood at home had been tense, but it had always been like that—at least as long as Lumikki could remember. She had never figured out where the tension came from, because she had never really seen Mom and Dad fighting or ever raised her own voice at them. As moving day got closer, her mother and father had given her frequent long hugs, which was strange and kind of irritating since that wasn't how their family was.

After the hugs, her mother would take Lumikki's face in her hands and look at her so long that it got a little weird.

"All we have is you. Only you."

Her mom kept repeating that, looking like she might burst

into tears at any second. Lumikki had started feeling harassed. When she finally got her belongings moved to Tampere with her parents' help, and closed the door for the first time after they left, she felt as if a heavy weight she didn't even know she was carrying had fallen off her shoulders.

"Are you really sure you're going to be okay here?"

Her mom always asked that. Her dad had a more practical approach.

"Flickan blir snart myndig. Hon måste ju klara sig," he would say, speaking Swedish to her instead of Finnish like he always did. And that was exactly what she was going to do. Daddy's grown-up *flicka* was going to fend for herself. A little better every day.

The girl who looked back at her in the bathroom mirror this morning was tired. The caffeine wasn't working its way through her body fast enough. Washing her face with cold water, Lumikki pulled her brown hair back in a ponytail. Her parents had stuck her with a name that had no connection to reality. Her hair wasn't black, her skin didn't shine like freshly fallen snow, and her lips weren't strikingly red. Seriously, who names their daughter after Snow White? It wasn't quite as bad in Finnish—Lumikki was an actual name, even if it was also the character in the Brothers Grimm story, but still. Why couldn't they have given her a Swedish name from Dad's side of the family? Of course she could have tried to make the image in the mirror match the name with some hair dye and makeup, but she didn't see any point in that. Her real reflection in the looking glass was good enough for her, and other people's opinions were irrelevant.

Lumikki thought about what to wear to school for

precisely three seconds. She decided to stick with the gray sweater and pull on some jeans. Combat boots, black wool jacket, green scarf and mittens, gray knit hat. Fjällräven backpack. Done.

Hunger gnawed at her stomach. Not even a light had greeted her in the empty refrigerator. The bulb had been broken for a couple of weeks, and she hadn't felt like changing it. She'd have to buy a sandwich from the snack bar at school. Maybe two. And definitely more coffee.

A familiar hectic clamor washed over her at the doors to the school. Everyone was in a hurry and needed to shout about what a hurry they were in. High school students were oh so articulate, so scintillating and creative in their modes of expression. Lumikki knew she was being mean, but some mornings, tolerating the colorful clothing and dramatic gestures was tough. And then there was the unspoken agreement everyone seemed to have about the lines they would stay inside so they could all be "different" and "unique" in the same damn way.

Underneath her irritation, Lumikki was thankful, though. Going to this school was a privilege. It meant she didn't have to be in Riihimäki anymore. Getting away from there had been the reason for applying here. Her parents might have had a hard time letting her move so far away to such a big city otherwise, but landing a prestigious spot in an elite magnet school for the arts was a good-enough excuse. And during her first few semesters, Lumikki felt like she had died and gone to heaven. That feeling had faded gradually, though, as she got used to the place and began to see how much jealousy, affectation, pretense, self-aggrandizement, and insecurity hid behind all the happy smiles.

Fortunately, the school wasn't just noisy, it was also warm, and Lumikki's stiff limbs began waking up. She knew the unbearable tingling was imminent, as the blood started circulating to her toes and fingers again. She should have put on two pairs of wool socks and crammed her feet into her boots. Tossing her coat onto a hook, Lumikki ran downstairs to the lunchroom and snack bar.

"Veggies today, or just plain?" the cook asked when she saw Lumikki.

"One of each, please," she replied. "And a large coffee."

"With no room for milk," the cook said with a laugh as she filled the paper cup to the brim.

Lumikki sat down at a table and let the warmth slowly sink into her body. Gah! The awful sensation was like a billion little needle pricks, but it was unavoidable in this weather. For a second, she thawed her hands against the coffee cup, and then took a bite of her sandwich. The roll was big and tasty, the tomato was ripe, and the bell pepper was crisp. Lumikki was a financial vegetarian. She didn't buy meat with her own money, but if someone else was buying and cooking some, then she was happy to eat it. Maybe that made her a hypocrite, but it worked.

Three girls assailed her eardrums from the next table. Blond hair was swung. Short dark hair was twirled. Red split ends were inspected. YSL Baby Doll, Britney Spears Fantasy, and Miss Dior Cherie wafted through the air.

"My head's going to explode if he treats me like I'm invisible today. If he thinks he can fool around with me at parties and then ignore me at school, he needs to think again. I can't believe he's already eighteen."

"My head feels like it's going to explode anyway. I should not have had those last few drinks. I don't even know what was in them!"

"Well, at least *we* were only drinking."

Feigned expressions of shock. Wide eyes.

"Oh my God, who?"

"Oh, come on. You would've had to be blind not to notice Elisa's pupils, dumbass. And she was totally jittery."

"She's always like that."

"This was like to the hundredth power."

Furtive glances. Three heads together, whispering. Lumikki drained her coffee cup and looked at the clock. Still ten minutes before first period. Standing, she took her plain roll and left. She couldn't deal with listening to the perfume mafia at the next table, and the smell was making her nauseated.

The school's social hierarchy was pretty simple.

There were the shallow girls who mostly cared about looks and wanted to get into law or business school. They came to the arts school because they had high GPAs and because they were, "you know, really creative and stuff."

There were the great Artists and even greater Intellectuals who saw school as a way to show off.

There were the math geniuses who always looked a little lost.

Then there were the normal, average kids who filled the halls, jammed the stairwells, formed endless lines in the cafeteria, and all looked, sounded, and smelled the same. No one would remember their names in a few years. No one even remembered them now.

There were also some smart kids who were actually nice, though. And usually, Lumikki didn't look down on the other kids either. She knew that the roles a lot of people played were just masks they put on at the beginning of each school day so that finding their place in the crowd would be easier. She didn't blame anyone for that. But on her very first day of high school, she'd decided that she wasn't going to let herself be forced into any category. She wasn't going to let anyone bundle her in with some group so people could make easy assumptions about her.

Lumikki had watched the formation of the divisions, the groupings, and the cliques with slight interest and mild amusement. She had stayed on the sidelines, on the outside. But she wasn't a loner freak either, sneaking along the walls dressed all in black. People remembered her name.

Lumikki Andersson. The Swedish-Finnish girl from Riihimäki. The one who had a carefully considered opinion about everything. The one who got perfect grades in physics *and* philosophy.

The one who had played Ophelia so well that two teachers got mad and the rest got all choked up.

The one who didn't participate in any of the school's pranks or parties.

The one who always ate alone, but never looked lonely.

She was the puzzle piece that didn't have its own place but could suddenly fill in almost any hole you needed it to.

She wasn't like the others.

She was exactly like the others.

Lumikki approached the darkroom's outer door and glanced both ways down the hall. No one around. Stepping inside the little vestibule, she pulled the door shut behind her. Darkness. Automatically, without fumbling, she reached forward and opened the inner door. Her hand knew the distance from memory. Impenetrable darkness. Silence. Peace. A moment to herself before the school day began. Meditating. Recharging. A daily ritual no one else knew about. A habit that was both an echo of the past and an integral part of the present. For so many years, Lumikki had needed to find hiding places because she was afraid. Finding secret nooks and safe havens was a lifeline. These days, it wasn't so much about fear as a desire to find some room just for her in a place that was shared by everyone. The darkroom was a refuge where she could collect herself for a few seconds before stepping out again into the middle of all those other people's talking and sounds and opinions and feelings.

Lumikki leaned against the wall and stared into the darkness with closed eyes, emptying her mind thought by thought. The easiest part was getting rid of the day-to-day, mostly trivial stuff that revolved around the coming math class, or maybe going to the grocery store after school, maybe going to Body Combat later. But today, for some reason, she couldn't get past the surface noise. Something pushed back. Something intruded.

A smell.

The darkroom smelled different than usual. But she couldn't quite place it. She took a step forward. Something gently brushed against her cheek and she jumped back, turning on the red safelight.

A five-hundred-euro bill.

Dozens of five-hundred-euro bills hanging in the darkroom to dry. Were they real? Lumikki touched the surface of the nearest one with her hand. The paper felt real, at least. She looked to make sure no photographs were developing in the processing trays and then turned on the normal light.

She squinted at the banknotes against the light. The watermarks were there, as were the see-through numbers. The security threads and holograms seemed to be in place. If the bills weren't genuine, they were extremely well-made forgeries.

The liquid in the processing trays was orange-brown. Lumikki tested it with a finger. Water.

Looking down at the darkroom floor, she saw that it was covered with reddish brown smudges. She stared in confusion at the corner of one fifty, which had the same russet tint. Then she knew what had disturbed her in the darkness.

The stench of old, dry blood.

4

LUMIKKI STARED OUT THE CLASSROOM WINDOW AT THE SPAR-kling, frosted trees and the old, small gravestones. But the white postcard landscape held no interest for her. Resting her eyes there was just easier than staring at the integral on the chalkboard since her mind wanted to work on something besides math.

She had left the cash in the darkroom. She had walked out, closed the door, and come straight to class. She hadn't said a word about it to anyone. One period to consider what to do.

The easiest way to get along in life is to meddle as little as possible.

That had been Lumikki's motto for years. No meddling, no messes, no sticking her nose in other people's business. If you were quiet and spoke only when you had something well-thought-out to say, you got to live in peace. Even now, she wanted simply to forget the whole business. Forget the banknotes washed clean of blood. Unfortunately, she knew that wasn't an option. The bills were already stuck in her mind just as firmly as the smell that clung to them. She knew they wouldn't leave her in peace until she did something to clear up the mystery.

She should probably tell the principal. That way, Lumikki could make it someone else's problem, put it out of her own thoughts. Maybe the money had something to do with some art project. But in that case, it couldn't be real. But why would someone have gone to so much trouble making play money? The bills looked so real that the police would be sure to consider them forgeries, and forgery was a crime.

Or maybe the bills were real.

Lumikki couldn't think of a single good reason why someone would have decided to clean that much money in the darkroom of the high school. And what's more, leave it there behind an unlocked door. It was ridiculous. Her brain churned, trying to find a logical explanation, but without success. She closed her eyes and saw the bills hanging from the drying lines. Some critical, decisive detail that would reveal the answer seemed to be missing from the picture in her mind. And it wasn't like she was some Sherlock Holmes who could take one look and then instantly reconstruct the convoluted chain of events that led up to tons of cash hanging in a school darkroom.

Lumikki had to talk to the principal. She should go and get the money and take it to the principal. Or should she not touch it?

The sun beat down on the branches of the trees, which

30

responded with a defiant glitter so dazzling it was painful to look at. Even in the warm classroom, Lumikki could hear the shrieking of the cold outside. She shivered. The stagnant air in the room was mind-numbing, and her thoughts plodded forward as if wading through thick goo.

Then she made a decision.

Lumikki walked toward the darkroom, wanting to confirm what she had seen. The whole scene had been so absurd that maybe she had imagined it. Or misunderstood. What if only one of the banknotes was real and the rest were just Monopoly money?

Never jump to conclusions. That was Lumikki's second motto.

Well, maybe calling them mottoes was too pretentious. They were more like principles or thoughts that had been useful or beneficial at some point.

Lumikki jumped when a boy walked around the corner. Tuukka. Eighteen years old, the son of the principal, a wannabe actor who thought he could play God's understudy if the call ever came. The teachers were amusingly adept at tolerating Tuukka's swaggering, arrogant manner of speaking and his chronic tardiness. Tuukka seemed to be in a hurry now, though. He probably would have shoved Lumikki with his elbow or backpack if she hadn't discreetly dodged him.

She had learned to sidestep without people noticing her sidestepping. You had to time it just right, and it had to be slight enough that it looked natural instead of like you were reacting to someone else. Lumikki had learned to be neither irritating nor obsequious.

Tuukka continued walking, speeding up almost to a run. He barely even noticed Lumikki. Still, best to wait until he disappeared before heading to the darkroom. Once she was sure he was really gone, Lumikki opened the outer door, closed it, opened the darkroom door, and turned on the red light.

Then she blinked two times.

The scene remained the same. The money was gone.

Lumikki cursed silently. This was what she got for not acting immediately. What was she going to do now? Go tell the principal that she had seen thousands of euros hanging in the darkroom without any way to prove it? Wait until someone asked her about it, and then describe what she'd seen? Forget the whole thing and chalk it up to a hallucination brought on by too little sleep and too much caffeine?

She leaned against the darkroom wall and closed her eyes. Something was bothering her again. Something out of place, something off. Her brain had recorded something, and now it was trying to figure out what didn't belong. Lumikki opened her eyes and realized what it was.

The backpack.

Tuukka never wore a backpack. He had a black leather Marimekko shoulder bag that could barely fit the books he needed on any given day. And when they didn't fit, he left some of them at home. Colorful fabric Marimekko bags were part of the standard uniform for high school girls, but Lumikki had never seen anyone with a leather one except Tuukka. As an accessory, it landed perfectly in the gray zone between conformity and individuality, a carefully considered move in step with the herd but with a subtle twist thrown in.

But Tuukka had been carrying a dingy gray backpack, frayed at the seams and stained at the corners, slung over one shoulder. Definitely not in keeping with the image of a demigod descended from on high to grace mere mortals with his presence. And it had been stuffed full without looking heavy.

Lumikki could solve this equation instantly.

The usual morning crowd was gathered at the Central Square Coffee House: mothers with their babies and mush and conversations about sleep schedules, college girls drinking lattes that gnawed gaping holes in their monthly budgets and pretending to study for exams while really daydreaming about the future, and a couple of men in suits with laptops playing Angry Birds or checking Facebook instead of working on their PowerPoints. Coffee machines whirring and gurgling. The scent of cappuccino and hazelnut syrup hanging in the air. Pastries that looked far more delicious than they really were. The sweat that came over you instantly when you walked in the door wearing a winter coat.

Lumikki sat at a corner table with her back to the rest of the café as she flipped through a magazine and drank her tea. At a nearby table sat Tuukka, Elisa, and Kasper.

Once Lumikki had realized that the cash was in Tuukka's backpack, she rushed after him immediately. She had snatched her coat, mittens, scarf, and knit hat from the coatrack. Running out of the school, she slipped and slid past the smoking spot and came to the churchyard, where she stopped and looked around for the boy. At the end of the park path, almost at Häme Street, she spotted the gray backpack swinging from his shoulder. Ignoring the cold air tearing at her lungs, Lumikki continued running, eventually slowing to a light jog and then a brisk walk to keep an appropriate distance. *See but don't be seen. Maintain line of sight.* Rules learned dodging playground tormenters had other applications too.

Her breathing, more like panting, went directly from vapor to icy glitter that stuck to her eyelashes and the locks of hair protruding from under her hat. In temperatures this far below zero, everyone's hair looked prematurely gray.

Lumikki had seen Tuukka enter the coffee house, and she waited a few minutes before following him inside. By then, the boy was already deep in conversation with Elisa and Kasper.

Now Lumikki was doing her best to remain invisible. Inconspicuous. Fortunately, she knew how to be someone else. Immediately upon entering, Lumikki had gone to the restroom, peeled off her outerwear and sweater, let down her hair, and arranged it in a side braid—a style she never wore. Instead of coffee, she ordered tea. She was browsing a women's magazine, although normally she'd have grabbed the sports pages or *Image* magazine. She sat in a different way, held her hands in a different position, tilted her head like someone else.

People thought they recognized each other from a distance based on clothing or hair. Superficially, that may have been true, but Lumikki knew that, in reality, recognizing another person was a much more complicated process influenced by hundreds or even thousands of different factors like height, posture, walk, bearing, body and face proportions, expressions, and even microexpressions that flitted by so fast they almost never registered consciously. That was why disguising yourself as someone else was so difficult. According to some people, it was actually impossible without significant plastic surgery and years of practice.

Still, surprisingly small changes could trim away your most recognizable characteristics if you knew what to do. If someone had been consciously looking for Lumikki, knowing that she was in there, of course they would have recognized her. But if you scanned the room expecting a crowd of strangers, Lumikki was just another slightly hippie-looking poet girl drinking chamomile tea. A girl with nothing conspicuously familiar about her.

So Tuukka, Elisa, and Kasper took no notice of Lumikki, even though they were sitting almost right next to her. After all, they had more important concerns. They had a problem.

"What should we do with it?" Elisa asked the boys.

As soon as she'd entered the coffee shop, Lumikki had noticed how terrible Elisa looked. Her skin was normally fair, but now it looked almost gray. She had dark rings under her eyes and had been careless when she washed or wiped off her last layer of makeup. Her bleached blond hair clung unwashed to her head. Instead of being stylish and coordinated, her clothing looked like she'd thrown on whatever her hand happened to land on first. Elisa would never have been caught dead looking like this at school. The fact that she had the nerve even to come to the coffee shop in such a state was startling.

Elisa was one of the most beautiful girls in school. She also acted the part, and her poise made everyone believe in her beauty even more strongly. Seeing her like this, exhausted and scared, you realized the beauty was a carefully constructed mask whose single most important factor was not the right color of lip gloss or professionally applied eye shadow, but a heavy dose of self-confidence and flirtatiousness. Elisa's smile made boys' hearts flutter and palms sweat.

To this day, Lumikki had never figured out the true nature of Elisa and Tuukka's relationship. Obviously, they had dated at some point, but now they seemed to be just friends. Maybe friends with benefits. Elisa toyed with the small male population of the arts high school as she saw fit, and of course, as a being descended from a higher sphere, Tuukka was most girls' fantasy, but some other glue seemed to bind them together too. Maybe they imagined that, as the alphas of the school, they were so far above everyone else that they could never seriously consider dating anyone else.

"What should we do? Duh. We should keep it, of course. Duh. And keep our mouths shut," Kasper said.

Lumikki wondered how Kasper had gotten into the school in the first place. He seemed to concentrate more on ditching class than doing homework. The whispers in the hall said he was on the verge of expulsion if things didn't change. Kasper dressed in black and wore flamboyant gold jewelry. Keeping his hair slicked back required a significant amount of gel, and in his world, he clearly thought he was some sort of bling-bling rap artist even though, in reality, his performances evoked more pity than excitement in the audience. Kasper was a weird dude, and you couldn't tell whether he was a chump or an actual small-time thug. For ages, Lumikki had wondered why Elisa and Tuukka hung out with Kasper at all. Elisa glanced around and lowered her voice.

"We can't keep it," she said.

The panic in her voice was audible.

"What do you think we should do then?" Tuukka asked. "Go tell the police?"

Kasper snickered. Elisa's dad was a cop. Occasionally, she received good-natured and sometimes less good-natured ribbing about that fact.

"It isn't ours. We ended up with it by accident, so someone out there is looking for it, and if they find us, we're screwed."

Elisa was desperate to convince the boys.

"Come on, Elisa, think. What can we really do? How can we explain everything that happened without getting in trouble? We should have told someone that night," Tuukka pointed out.

"We did do something," Kasper said, snickering.

Elisa sighed. "Yeah. We acted like regular geniuses."

"It seemed logical at the time," Tuukka said. "But you get what I'm saying. If we tell about the . . . it . . . we have to tell about everything else. And I don't know about you, but I can't risk that."

"Neither can I," Kasper said.

Lumikki heard Elisa's fingernails drumming nervously on the tabletop as she spoke.

"My memory's way too fuzzy to say anything for sure. I can't even sort out what happened when. Mostly I just know that my house was a god-awful mess in the morning. You don't even want to hear all the places I found puke."

"I bet you've got a lot of scrubbing to do so your dad doesn't realize you weren't just sitting at home studying phys-ics all weekend."

Kasper leaned back in his chair with an amused look on his face.

"Are you crazy? Today's when the maid comes. She's cleaning everything up right now. I promised to pay her double if she does it in half the usual time and keeps her mouth shut. If I could just remember everything that happened, maybe I could—"

"Get us all in really, really big trouble? That sounds like an awesome plan."

Tuukka's voice had a hard, threatening edge to it.

Elisa was silent for a moment. At the next table, someone made it to the next level on Angry Birds and gave a satisfied "Yes!"

"Okay, fine," Elisa said. "We'll keep our mouths shut. For now. We'll wait and see what happens. But I have to say, I have a really bad feeling about this."

"Maybe ten grand will make you feel better," Tuukka said.

"What? No, I don't want any."

"Of course you do. I've got three bags. Ten thousand each. We're all in this together."

There was some rustling and the sound of a zipper as Tuukka opened his backpack under the table. Lumikki turned her head slightly and watched out of the corner of her eye as two opaque black plastic bags were transferred from Tuukka's backpack to Elisa's and Kasper's bags.

Elisa pressed her face into her hands and gave an anguished sigh.

"Fuck. This morning, when I woke up, I was so hoping this was all just a bad dream."

"No one saw you, did they?" Kasper asked Tuukka.

"No."

"And no one had gone in the darkroom?" Kasper asked.

"And just left all that there? I seriously doubt it."

But there was tension in Tuukka's laugh. Suddenly, he stood up.

"This meeting is over. You can leave now."

"I'm still drinking my chai," Elisa said.

"If I was you, I wouldn't hang around town looking like that any longer than I had to," Tuukka said. "And I mean that with all the love in the world, baby."

"Yeah. You're one to talk," Elisa threw back, but she did get up.

Lumikki waited until the trio left. Then she tried to gulp down the rest of her tea. God. Did people really drink this stuff voluntarily? She ended up leaving the dregs of the over-priced dishwater in her cup. When a safe amount of time had passed, she bundled up and stepped back out into the biting cold. She'd have time to think on the way home.

5

A BITTER, ELECTRIC COLD WIND WAS BLOWING ACROSS THE stone bridge over the rapids that ran through the middle of the city. Lumikki hurried her steps, processing what she had heard. Tuukka, Elisa, and Kasper had somehow ended up with the money last night. How, Lumikki didn't know. Whose money was it? Did they even know? Maybe not. Probably not. They seemed more confused than usual about what had happened the night before.

The money had obviously been bloody already, and the three of them had come up with the genius idea of washing it in the school darkroom. That was the hardest part to understand. Who would ever think to go to school in the middle of the night to clean a pile of dirty money?

At least we were only drinking.

Suddenly, the words of the perfume mafia echoed in

Lumikki's head. So people must have been doing more than just drinking at the party last night. Some of them, at least. Maybe Elisa, Tuukka, and Kasper. That might explain why they'd come up with such a ridiculous solution. And it would also explain why they couldn't tell anyone about what happened.

A policeman's daughter. A principal's son. The scenario was so classic it made Lumikki shake her head. Kids from good families desperate to be rebellious? Playing dangerous games with drugs and alcohol and who knew what else because they couldn't get enough excitement from anything else? Or did they just want to get really messed up?

People were sliding all over the place at the intersection by the train station. No amount of gravel the city spread around was enough to ensure traction in a place where thousands of pairs of feet polished the ice every day. Lumikki let her combat boots slap harder on the ground.

The situation had gotten significantly more complicated. She didn't want to go talk to the principal now. Or the police. She didn't want to get involved at all, even though the trio weren't her friends in any way. They didn't mean anything to her, but she definitely didn't want to end up in the middle of the shit storm that was sure to blow up if she snitched.

An anonymous tip to the police? That was definitely an option. Would they take it seriously? Probably, if someone had reported thirty thousand euros missing. And if they didn't take her seriously, it wouldn't be her problem anymore. She would have done her duty.

As she approached Tammela, Lumikki felt a strange surge

of emotion. Her apartment wasn't really home, no question there, but maybe she'd started to warm up to the neighborhood? The thought amused her. Black sausage and milk at Tammela Square. The cheers of soccer fans from the Tammela Stadium. Basic stuff all the locals did. Nostalgia for the few wooden buildings left from old Tammela and admiration for the red brick buildings of the former Aaltonen Shoe Factory. That didn't sound at all like Lumikki Andersson, who avoided all that mushy stuff. Still, for some reason, she felt a little more relaxed and a little warmer here than in other parts of town. Hometown pride wasn't in her vocabulary, but there were probably worse things in the world than liking where you lived. Maybe this neighborhood could become her home. Maybe she could start thinking of these streets as her own. Maybe that had already started to happen, even though Lumikki didn't consciously want to get too attached to any one place.

The shouts and laughter and cries of children echoed from the yard of the Tammela School. Lumikki watched as the girls and boys ran and jumped and swung and climbed, their breath steaming and their cheeks red from the cold. In their thick winter clothing, they were like pudgy, colorful snowmen. Her gaze scanned the edges of the schoolyard for the lonely children abandoned by their peers. She focused her ears to pick out the cries of fear from the shouts of joy. Lumikki knew that, for some, this schoolyard glittering in the winter sun was a nightmare kingdom where the days were as long and black as night.

A little girl walked around the lemon-colored art nouveau school building by herself. She trudged, head held down.

Lumikki watched the girl for a moment. Did she turn at each corner to glance behind her? Did she flinch every now and then? Was that anguish in her downcast eyes? No. When Lumikki could finally make out the girl's face, she found her smiling. The girl's lips were moving. She was probably creating a story in her mind that made her eyes smile along.

She isn't like I was then, Lumikki thought. Thank goodness.

Then she realized that something was amiss. Something was wrong. Someone was too close.

She realized too late.

Suddenly, strong hands grabbed her and dragged her into the shadows of a nearby doorway, shoving her violently against the stone wall. Lumikki's cheek pressed hard against the frigid rock. The surprise attack left Lumikki's arms limp as her assailant pulled them painfully behind her back. Lumikki barely managed to contain a yelp.

She recognized her attacker from his smell before he said a single word.

Tuukka.

"You're not the only one who knows how to tail someone."

Tuukka's words came with an unpleasant warmth on her cheek. His breath stank of the coffee he had just drunk and a recently smoked cigarette. Lumikki was furious with herself. How could she have made such a rookie mistake? How could she have left the coffee shop without watching her back?

Never overestimate your own cleverness. Never think you are completely safe. She should know better by now. Her skills had grown rusty in Tampere since she didn't need them every day anymore. No one bullied her now.

"I spotted you in the coffee shop. Well, not you, just this backpack of yours. And then I realized that I almost ran into you back by the darkroom. Quite a coincidence, isn't it?" Tuukka said, squeezing Lumikki's arm.

Lumikki quickly evaluated the situation.

If she moved fast enough, she might be able to wrench free of Tuukka's grasp. That wasn't guaranteed, though. And Tuukka was fast. He would just catch her again. Better not to struggle and waste her strength for no reason. She might as well hear what he had to say.

"What did you see? What do you know?" Tuukka asked.

"I saw the darkroom earlier. And I heard what you were saying in the café. That's all," Lumikki replied calmly.

Provoking him now wasn't going to get her anywhere.

"Damn it," Tuukka said. "Nobody can know about this."

Lumikki did not reply. The rough, icy stone of the wall chafed her cheek. She tried to move as little as possible.

"You're going to keep your mouth shut. You aren't going to tell anyone. You don't know anything. No one would even believe you."

Tuukka tried to sound menacing, but there was uncertainty in his voice. Lumikki still didn't say a word.

"Do you hear me?"

Tuukka's voice was louder and even more uncertain. He was afraid. He was much more afraid than Lumikki was.

"I hear you," Lumikki said.

Tuukka thought for a second.

"Okay. How much do you want?" he asked.

Now his voice was almost pleading. He was clearly worried about what all this could do to his reputation.

"I don't want any of it," Lumikki replied. "But now you're going to let me go."

It wasn't a request or a command, simply a statement. A fact. Never give people options, just give them simple directives. Don't beg or demand, just tell them how things are. Lumikki's certainty made Tuukka release his grip, and she turned, slowly massaging her wrists.

"Now, this is what we're going to do," she said, looking the boy firmly in the eye. "I have zero desire to get mixed up in this. I didn't see anything, and I didn't hear anything. I'm not going to go looking to rat on anyone, but if someone asks me directly, I'm also not going to lie. I think you're going to get into trouble over this, and I have no intention of saving you."

Tuukka looked at her hesitantly. His ears were red from the cold. He wasn't wearing a hat. Vanity seemed to trump practicality. He was clearly considering Lumikki's words, weighing the risks and his options.

"Okay. It's a deal," he said finally, extending his hand.

Lumikki didn't take it. Tuukka ran it through his hair and laughed.

"You're a surprisingly tough chick. Maybe I underestimated you."

Lots of people do, Lumikki thought.

Trying to regain the upper hand, Tuukka presumptuously brushed Lumikki's hair out of her face.

"You know what? You could actually be pretty goodlooking if you changed this horrible hair, ditched those Greenpeace clothes, and learned to put on makeup," he said, curling one corner of his mouth.

Lumikki smiled.

"And do *you* know what?" she replied. "You could actually be a pretty smart, nice guy if you completely changed
your horrible personality."

She didn't hang around to hear what Tuukka might say
to that, just walked away, not looking back. She knew he
wouldn't follow her.

Back at her apartment, Lumikki looked in the mirror at
her red tingling cheek. The mark was going to be visible for
at least a day. It was small, though, and she had experienced
much worse. Drinking some cold water straight from the tap,
she decided not to go to school the next day. She could afford
to stay home this one time. Then everything would be normal again. She would go to school. She would forget about
the money. She wouldn't get involved in any way.

TUESDAY, MARCH 1

6

IT WAS 3:45 A.M.

Boris Sokolov was staring at his cell phone like it was an oversized cockroach, fantasizing about smashing it against the wall. The call had woken him in the middle of a dream. He had been lied to. He had been threatened. Now, he could tolerate being woken up. The lying disgusted him. But what Boris Sokolov truly hated was being threatened. Especially by a man who shouldn't have been in any position to make threats.

Boris Sokolov switched out his cell phone's SIM card and dialed a number.

After three rings, the Estonian answered. Boris could tell the call had woken him too. The Estonian's voice sounded viscous and distant, even though he lived only a few miles away.

"Well?"

Boris began speaking to the Estonian in Russian. "He called. He says he never got the money."

"He's crazy," the Estonian said. "We took it right to his house."

Boris got out of bed and walked to the bedroom window. The parquet floor felt cold. Maybe he should have put carpet in. Who cared if it got dirty? He could just have it replaced every couple of years. The moonlight was unpleasantly bright. Two sets of rabbit tracks crossed in the yard. The Estonian had helped him cover up another kind of tracks, tramping a natural-looking path to the other side of the backyard. Carefully removing any snow that wasn't perfectly white.

"He said he waited up all night. Tonight."

"What the hell? We told him it was coming at the usual time but a different place."

The Estonian was starting to really wake up now.

Boris grunted. "He said something about a misunderstanding. That yesterday was leap day and the last day of the month."

He tapped his fingers on the windowsill. Had the rabbits been gnawing at the apple tree? He would have to rig up some sort of fencing around it. Or keep watch one night and score a couple of rabbit roasts for the freezer. His own freezer this time.

"Yeah, yeah, but the twenty-eighth doesn't turn into the twenty-ninth because of leap year. And why the hell was he waiting up tonight when we already delivered the money yesterday?"

"That's just it. He says we didn't. That he hasn't seen anything. Nada."

The Estonian was silent for a moment. Boris waited to see

whether his underling would come to the same conclusion he had.

"He's bullshitting us. He did get the money. He just realized what happened to it, and now he's trying to play hardball."

Yep, same conclusion.

"The little shit tried to threaten me. He said he'd expose everything."

Boris felt himself getting angry again just saying the words. He squeezed the cell phone, imagining the crunch of a cockroach exoskeleton in his fist.

"But I'll burn in hell before I see that!"

The Estonian was furious too. Good. They were firmly on the same side. Two backsliders within the past thirty-eight hours was enough. No, it was too much. Two too many. A working machine could only lose so many parts at a time without repairs.

"We're going to make sure he doesn't talk."

Boris said the words with relish. No one threatened him without repercussions. No one bullshitted him and got away with it.

He had thought a plastic bag full of bloody cash would have been sufficient warning.

Apparently not.

But he knew how to play hardball too. The difference was he would win.

Terho Väisänen knew there was no way he was going to fall back asleep. He lay on one side of the queen-sized bed, even though he could have stretched out across the whole mattress if he'd wanted to. He felt as if someone were whittling the bed frame out from under him and that at any moment he might collapse onto the floor, which would also give way. Something was crumbling, something he had thought would last.

Terho Väisänen couldn't say he was proud of himself. There were mornings when he had a hard time looking himself in the eye, but usually the feeling went away by the time he got to work and remembered how much good he had done over the past ten years. How many cases had been solved solely thanks to him? That kind of success rate had its price, but so be it.

Pulling the covers up around his neck, he sniffed the fresh scent of the duvet cover. He wished he could hug someone, hold someone warm tight in his arms.

Terho tried to call one more time. The phone rang and rang, but no one answered. Terho felt a vague fear taking root somewhere around his solar plexus. He had a feeling that, after tonight, everything would be different.

7

ONCE UPON A TIME, THERE WAS A NIGHT THAT NEVER ENDED. With its darkness, it devoured the sun, strangling all light and spreading its cold black hands over the earth. The night glued the eyes of humanity shut eternally, making dreams deeper and stranger, making man and woman alike forget themselves and glide along arm in arm with imagined creatures, losing their own memories. On the walls of the buildings, the night painted its most terrifying pictures, from which all color had fled. On the faces of the sleeping populace, the night breathed cold, suffocating air, which invaded the lungs, turning them black inside.

Gasping, Lumikki opened her eyes. She was covered in sweat, and the weight of her quilt felt like it was choking her throat. She had to throw it off and sit up. Feet shoved into slippers. Over to the window to look out across the park, a familiar scene that could soften the rock-hard anxiety of the nightmare until it was just an uneasy, hollow feeling. The moon illuminated the snowbanks, the playground swings and jungle gym, and the roofs of the buildings, wrapping them all in a silvery skin. The shadows stood in place like figures painted black on the snow.

Light shone from the windows of two different apartments. Someone else was awake this morning at 3:45 a.m. A perverse time to be awake, against human nature. Only the nightmare images of dreams were abroad at this hour, indistinguishable to the human eye from the other shadows. The bottom edge of the window was decorated in a lace of frost flowers. Instinctively, Lumikki touched the cold glass, even though she knew the ice crystals were on the other side. The warmth of her hand couldn't melt them. Cold air breathed on her fingers through a chink in the window frame. Lumikki pulled her hand back and shivered.

There had been a time when she would wake up hoping the night would never end and the morning would never come. She'd dreamed of endless nights back then as well, but those had been hopeful dreams. Now they were nightmares. Many things had changed. Back then, Lumikki would wake up in the morning disappointed to have to get up and face another day that was unlikely to bring anything good. She knew there would be more evil on offer than a normal person could endure. But she did endure—she endured for years on end. Maybe she was as abnormal as they had claimed.

Lumikki returned to her covers and warm bed. Exhaustion pressed her eyelids shut, and she didn't have any more bad dreams all night. She didn't dream any dreams at all, at least none that she remembered the next day.

★   ★   ★

Lumikki awoke again to the sun shining. It was already after ten. Her whole body felt oddly rested and refreshed. This must have been how people were supposed to feel in the morning, not like a zombie woken from the dead for the umpteenth time. She wasn't usually one for skipping school, but this time it had probably been a good idea. She didn't want to see Tuukka's smug face again this soon.

Lumikki stretched out her legs and arms on the bed. What should she do today? Maybe go to the gym. Her aunt Kaisa had bought her a year membership at a fitness center for Christmas. Lumikki didn't exactly feel at home surrounded by all the perky aerobics girls, but sweating always did her good, and she needed to build muscle. Tuukka had succeeded in surprising her and momentarily getting the upper hand. But if Lumikki could have trusted in her physical strength, breaking away and giving him a taste of his own cheek smashed against the cold rock wall would have been easy.

Do not seek power for revenge. Seek power in order to avoid situations that would make you want revenge. That sounded noble. In reality, all it meant was that Lumikki never wanted to be at a disadvantage ever again.

She didn't want to think about the previous day. She just wanted to think about today. Her day.

Her mom and her aunt went on and on sometimes about how important it was for women to take time to pamper themselves. "Pampering" being a synonym for shopping, chocolate, bubble baths, women's magazines, and nail polish.

Lumikki shuddered. For her, a day like that wouldn't be pampering; it would be an awkward charade.

For her, a day of pampering meant comic books, black licorice, serious exercise, veggie curry, and above all, solitude. Her mom always wondered how she could get along so well alone. Didn't she ever get bored? Lumikki didn't bother saying that she was more likely to get bored being around other people, listening to their pointless small talk. Better off alone than in bad company. When she was alone, she could be completely herself. Free. No one demanding anything. No one talking when she wanted silence. No one touching her when she didn't want to be touched.

Lumikki also enjoyed going to art shows. She would set aside several hours, load her phone with enough music, preferably Massive Attack, and go without any preconceptions, trying not to learn too much ahead of time about the artist or the exhibition theme. After paying the admission fee, she would enter the gallery staring at the floor, turn on her headphones, and close her eyes. She would empty her thoughts, filling her head with music. She would concentrate on breathing evenly and let her heart rate slow down. Once she had made the surrounding world disappear, she would open her eyes and fall into the first piece.

Sometimes she completely lost her sense of time. Pictures, colors, moods, the feeling of movement on the canvas or paper or photograph, the sense of depth, the irregularity and texture of the surface would drag her deep into a world she didn't completely recognize or understand, but which was still hers. Other Finns had their lakes and forests, but this was the landscape of Lumikki's soul. Art spoke to her in a language that intermingled with music, forming pathways that led to darkness or light. The subjects weren't important to her. What the pictures depicted or whether they depicted anything at all mattered even less. All that mattered was the feeling.

Lumikki rarely left a show without getting something out of it. Sometimes that did happen, but usually the reason was an external factor like hunger or fatigue or stress. Or other people being disruptive and making so much noise her music couldn't completely drown them out. Some shows were like tornadoes that she left gasping for air and trying to regain her balance. Some she felt as a heat in her chest for days afterward. Some reverberated in her head. The colors persisted on the retinas of her eyes, painting new shades on her dreams. She was never the same person after a show as she was before.

Today wasn't going to be an art day, though, because Lumikki had already been to see all the traveling exhibitions at the Tampere Museum of Art, the Sara Hildén Art Museum, and the TR1 Kunsthalle, and their permanent collections were old news. She usually tried to make it to a show early on, but not during the very first weeks. After the hardcore art groupies were out of the way and the wannabes were still at home on the couch.

The sun made the frost flowers on the window glitter. Lumikki reconsidered the idea of going for a short jog before breakfast. She looked at the thermometer, which said it was thirteen degrees below zero. No thanks. Breathing hard would be too much for her lungs.

Suddenly, her cell phone rang. Lumikki picked it up. She didn't recognize the number.

Don't answer unfamiliar numbers. Not ever. That had been

her motto before, but not anymore. These days, she had to have the courage to answer those calls too, since she lived alone and handled all her own affairs.

"Lumikki Andersson," she said in a formal tone.

"Hi, it's Elisa."

Elisa? Why would Elisa be calling her?

"Tuukka told me that you know," the girl continued quickly.

Lumikki sighed. She wouldn't have to convince Elisa that she wasn't going to go looking to tell anyone too, would she?

"I didn't know who else to call. The boys don't want to talk about what happened. I'm totally losing it. You have to come here. I can't stand being alone. I'm afraid. Help me."

Elisa's voice was high-pitched, frantic. She was clearly panicking.

"Well, I don't know—" Lumikki began, but she couldn't get any further before Elisa broke down in sobs.

Lumikki stared at the frost flowers. What if she just pressed the red "end" button? And then switched off the phone? *Don't get involved. Don't interfere. Only worry about your own business.* Why was sticking to her mottoes so difficult now? Maybe because Elisa was crying. Maybe because no one had ever asked for her help so directly before.

Lumikki couldn't believe it when she heard herself say into the phone, "Okay, I'll come over." So much for a day on her own.

Elisa lived in Pyynikki, across the river at the base of a large, elongated hill that looked out over the city of Tampere and its surrounding lakes. The most expensive neighborhood in the city. Lumikki felt completely out of place standing at the front gate in her shabby winter coat. A stone wall separated the large front yard from the street. At the back of the property rose the hill, which was famous for its forested walking paths. White and stately, the house itself was shockingly large. Lumikki had always imagined that at least two families must live in each of these buildings, but apparently that wasn't true, at least in this case. There weren't any names visible anywhere, as if the residents of these homes feared their mailboxes giving away too much about them.

One more peek at the text message. Yes, she had the right address.

Two bronze lions sat atop the stone gateposts. Each held a bronze ball protectively under its paw. *Beware of lions.*

Lumikki pressed the buzzer. Within seconds, Elisa opened the front door and rushed down to the gate in some sort of pink fleece tracksuit. Lumikki might be wearing old, threadbare clothes from a thrift shop, but at least she didn't look like an escapee from a mental hospital. Elisa opened the gate and threw her arms around Lumikki before she could dodge out of the way.

"Thank you so much for coming! I wasn't sure how you'd react since we don't know each other that well," Elisa blubbered.

She smelled of roses and affluence. Lumikki didn't wear perfume herself, but she had trained her nose to identify different brands. She had actually become pretty good at it. There was a time when identifying a person at a distance based only on their perfume had given her the decisive extra seconds she needed to escape.

"Joy by Jean Patou," she observed as she quickly extricated herself from the hug. The recent cultural innovation in Finland of hugging strangers was like a stubborn cold requiring a speedy remedy.

Elisa looked at Lumikki in astonishment. "I didn't know you were into perfume. I got this one last Christmas from my dad. They say it's the world's most expensive scent."

"Yeah."

Lumikki had absolutely no desire to get tangled up in some pointless conversation about perfume and Christmas presents. No small talk. She had come because Elisa had been panicked and crying. If she was just here to be some sort of lap dog, she could turn around and go back home right now. She could still make it to Body Combat class.

Elisa was bouncing around like an overstimulated pink bunny. She didn't seem to have realized until now how tightly the temperature held them in its grip.

"Let's go inside," she said.

Lumikki nodded.

The house was even more beautiful inside than out. High ceilings, bay windows, blond wood, pieces of furniture that clearly cost more than Lumikki paid in rent in a year, lots of winter sunshine spilling over the floors and other surfaces without revealing a single particle of dust. The maid Elisa had mentioned in the coffee shop the day before had done excellent work for her double pay.

"Downstairs is the sauna and pool area," Elisa felt the need to report as Lumikki removed her black boots and coat, tossing her mittens, scarf, and stocking cap on the shelf above the coat hooks.

"I didn't come here to swim," she replied curtly.

Elisa was abashed. "Of course not. Sorry. Do you want anything? Cappuccino, mochaccino, latte?"

"Just regular coffee. Black."

"Okay. I'll get it. You can go up and wait in my room."

Lumikki started walking up the stairs. On the landing was a mirror where she glanced at this out-of-place girl. What the hell was she doing here? Agreeing to come had been a mistake. Despite herself, she was getting sucked deeper and deeper into a swamp that smelled worse by the minute.

Elisa's room looked like something pink and black had exploded in it. The two colors dominated everything from the rugs to the walls, from the curtains to the laptop. Was this some sort of extended princess phase with a little punk rock sprinkled on top for street cred? The bedroom was twice the size of Lumikki's studio apartment. There was also a door out to a small balcony.

Elisa seemed to have an endless array of jewelry and makeup. The bookshelf was full of horror movies and romantic comedies.

Lumikki looked for a flaw in the room. Every person's room had a flaw, something that didn't fit, that contradicted the impression they were trying to give.

There were two flaws in Elisa's room.

On the lowest shelf of the bookcase was a row of books on astronomy. They had been shoved down there as if to keep them out of sight, but there were enough of them that they couldn't just be left over from a single failed gift or there by chance. And now Lumikki remembered that Elisa had always excelled in math and physics.

The second flaw was a plump ball of yarn and knitting needles with the beginnings of a sweater or something on them. So Elisa didn't want everything to be perfect and store-bought.

Interesting. Or it would have been if Lumikki had felt any desire to get to know Elisa. Now she simply registered these irregularities and tucked them away in her mind.

"Coffee, black!" Elisa announced at the door and handed Lumikki a mug.

It was black. Elisa's own cup was pink. This observation amused Lumikki momentarily. But the sociological fieldwork could end right there.

"Why did you ask me to come here?" she asked.

Elisa flopped down on her bed and sighed. "I'm so afraid, and I don't know what I should do."

"What do you remember about the night of the party?"

"Not much. Or, I mean, I remember lots of things, but I'm having a hard time connecting any of them."

"Tell me from the very beginning, in as much detail as possible, what you remember about the party and how you ended up with the money," Lumikki suggested. "Then we can think about the best course of action."

She hated the didactic tone in her voice, but right now she had to talk to Elisa like a child. The girl's hands were shaking, even though she was squeezing her cup tightly to make them stop.

Slowly, Elisa began telling her story, which was so full of digressions that it was almost incoherent. After learning that her parents would be out of town Sunday night, she'd decided to throw a party. Her mother was leaving on Saturday for a weeklong business trip, and her father would be gone overnight, also for work. Elisa droned on for a while about all the thought she'd put into who to invite and what food and drinks to get. *Get to the point,* Lumikki thought. This wasn't exactly what she meant by detail. If she wanted to gossip, Elisa could find another listener.

"I wanted my party to have a little more sparkle. So I asked Kasper to get some pills for me and Tuukka. We've taken them together before. You get a way better buzz than from alcohol. And too many drinks always make me want to puke."

Elisa's sullen expression amused Lumikki. Who didn't have to puke after drinking too much? Wasn't that one of the basic features of alcohol?

"Where did Kasper score them?" she asked.

"I don't know. And I don't wanna know. Sometimes he runs with a sketchy crowd that it's best to avoid."

A sudden virtuous tone. Elisa seemed to be remembering that she was the daughter of a police officer.

"Did anyone else take them?"

"Not that I know of. Kasper is pretty careful about who he deals to. He doesn't want to get caught."

Of course he doesn't. But Lumikki could have told Elisa that at least the perfume mafia seemed to know perfectly well that people had been partying with more than alcohol.

"Most people started going home around midnight." Elisa laughed. "Good little kiddies don't want to be too hung over at school the next day."

When Lumikki didn't join in the laughter, Elisa turned serious too.

"Okay, now that I look back on it, I should have stopped

then too. Everybody who stuck around was pretty drunk by that point. I know I was super messed up, and that's when my memory gets fuzzy. Some people were puking in the corners. Someone broke a crystal vase and got cut on the glass. The whole house was a wreck. I think I asked Tuukka to throw a couple of idiots out."

Elisa had lowered her coffee cup to her desk. She started picking at her cuticles. Her bright pink nail polish was worn off at the tips. Her hands still trembled slightly. Lumikki didn't say anything. Better to let Elisa tell her story without any leading questions. Memories were more reliable without someone else prompting them.

"By two, everyone had left except Tuukka and Kasper. We were mostly up here in my room hanging out. We didn't have to pretend anymore that we were just drinking. Then . . . it was around three o'clock."

Elisa suddenly fell silent. She swallowed, then frowned.

"I think I went out on the balcony to smoke," she continued. "Yeah, that's right. And I saw this weird plastic trash bag down in the garden. It had been there half an hour, max, because I kept going out to smoke and that's the first time I saw it. I don't usually smoke, but at parties I always just, like, really want a couple cigarettes."

Again, the same virtuous tone and role-playing mask. Lumikki would have admired the performance if it hadn't irritated her so much.

"What did you do then?" she asked, unable to restrain herself.

Elisa started fiddling with the gold heart dangling from the zipper of her pink tracksuit. She pulled it down a couple of inches and then jerked it up again. Open and shut. Open and shut. Lumikki took a sip of coffee. It was painfully weak. "For some reason, I started laughing hysterically because the bag looked so weird sitting there in the snow. I can't explain it. I guess I was really messed up. I left the boys upstairs and went to get the bag. When I came inside, I opened it down in the hall."

Elisa swallowed again. "At first, I didn't understand what it was. I thought it was trash. Then I pulled out one of the pieces of paper and realized it was money. Covered in blood. The whole bag was full of bloody five-hundred-euro bills. I dug around to check, and my hands got all covered in the blood. Thinking about it makes me sick. But when it was happening, I just kept laughing. Somehow it was ridiculously funny."

Elisa stared at the pink rug on the black floor. The emotions on her face ran from nausea to disgust and from shame to fear.

"I didn't think at all about why the money was ... like that. I yelled for the boys to come and look. They started laughing too and saying over and over, 'We're all fucking rich now.' We didn't count it then, but the bag had thirty thousand euros in it. We weren't actually thinking at all. Yeah, you know, except that we had to clean the money somehow."

They had reasoned that they couldn't wash it at anyone's house since they wouldn't be able to let it dry without someone noticing. Then Tuukka came up with the darkroom idea because he took photography. And he had a copy of his dad's key to the school he had made a long time ago. And he knew the code to the building alarm.

"It felt like the smartest idea in the world at the time,"

Elisa explained, looking at Lumikki with pleading eyes. "Can you understand?"

No, Lumikki thought, but she didn't say so out loud. "And in the morning, Tuukka had to hurry to get the money out of there," she said instead.

"As far as I'm concerned, we should have left it there. I never wanted to touch it again. I can't stop thinking about where all that blood came from. Was it from a person? And why was the bag in my yard? Who put it there? I'm never taking any fucking pills ever again. If I had been sober, I might have seen who brought the bag."

Elisa stood up and started pacing nervously.

Lumikki stood up as well, going to the balcony door and opening it. Cold air immediately assaulted her, but she didn't care. She went out on the balcony and looked down into the yard.

"Was the gate down there locked that night?" she asked.

"Yes," Elisa replied. "I checked it around two, I think."

Lumikki estimated the distance from the road to the yard. With a nice strong throw, it would be easy enough to toss a trash bag over the stone fence.

"Is there a security camera on the street?"

Elisa shook her head.

"There's one at the gate and at the door, but not on the street."

Lumikki thought. She let the sharp air nibble at her fingers. It kept her mind alert.

Someone had thrown a bag full of blood-soaked money over Elisa's garden wall in the middle of the night. The money pointed to a payment. The blood pointed to a warning. *So was the money a threat or a thank-you? And who was it for? Had they thrown the bag into the right yard?*

Viewed from the street, the house to the right looked very different, and the yard extended farther out. The road made a small turn at Elisa's house, which was set farther back, in a corner where the street split into two.

"Who lives there?" Lumikki asked, indicating the house to the right.

"Two families with little kids. I think both moms are lawyers or something. One of the dads is some kind of artist, and the other one works for the city. Their kids aren't in school yet."

Lumikki sized up the duplex and yard. Confusing it with Elisa's house seemed unlikely. However, the house to the left, although clearly newer, was similar in size, shape, and color. Even the wall was an identical continuation of the one in front of Elisa's family's. Someone could easily have mixed them up in the middle of the night.

"What about that one?"

Elisa was standing next to her on the balcony now, shivering.

"Oh, him? He's a total weirdo. He's like forty or something, but he tries to look younger. It's like he's trying to reenact *Twilight* because he dresses in these long leather coats. He must think he looks like some kind of prince of the vampires or something. Really, he just looks pathetic. I don't have a clue what he does. He must work somewhere, though, because every morning he goes out and then comes back at night. He lives alone in that big house, and I've never seen anyone visiting. He doesn't even say hi on the street."

Lumikki looked at Elisa, whose eyes went wide.

"The money must have been meant for him! It just ended up in the wrong yard! He's totally the type to be mixed up in some shady deals or animal sacrifices or something." Elisa almost sounded pleased.

"That's one possibility," Lumikki said, "but not the only one."

If the money *had* been thrown into the right yard, then the intended recipient was Elisa, her father, or her mother.

Lumikki glanced at Elisa, whose teeth were beginning to chatter. She was like a stuffed animal that had lost most of its stuffing, shivering in the cold. Hard to believe she could be involved in anything that would result in a thirty-thousand-euro payoff. Of course, you never knew. Lumikki considered herself better than average at spotting liars. Elisa didn't seem like a liar. At least, not a good-enough one to be able to fool her. Lumikki had been lied to so many times in her life that she could pick out the changes in tone and expression that exposed most mediocre liars.

"Still, I have a bad feeling someone out there wants that money back right now," Elisa whispered.

Lumikki had nothing comforting to say.

She agreed completely.

8

VIIVO TAMM SHIVERED. HE COULDN'T REMEMBER THE LAST time he'd been so cold. He tried to bounce in place to keep warm, but his stiff leg muscles wouldn't cooperate.

He'd only been standing at his post along the Pyynikki Hill running path for an hour, but he already felt like he was running up against the limits of what he could tolerate. He had on a thick parka with a tightly woven sweater underneath and a Thinsulate cap pulled down over his ears, but the cold was still finding a way through the layers. It attacked through the smallest needle holes, mercilessly gnawing at his body, which was struggling desperately to maintain a safe core temperature. Viivo Tamm gave in and made the call.

Stiff fingers poked clumsily at the equally stiff buttons of the cell phone. Removing his lined leather gloves wasn't an option. Extracting the correct name from the contact list and pressing the green "call" icon felt like it took minutes.

"Well?" came the expectant reply.

"No sign. And I can't stay out here much longer. I'm freezing to death."

"Suck it up," Boris Sokolov snapped, and hung up.

Viivo stared at the phone for a second, clenching his teeth. Sokolov and Linnart Kask were sitting in a plumbing company van at the far end of the street. It was all well and good for them to be issuing orders while sitting there nice and toasty warm.

What if the girl didn't come out today? Or even just not very soon? All three of them knew they couldn't keep up the stakeout for hours on end. Someone would notice the van and get suspicious. They'd realize that no one around here needed a plumber right now. Switching out the vehicle's license plate and logos would cost time and money, and none of them wanted to do that any more than they had to.

Fucking hell. They had been sure that seeing the blood would be enough. But this guy had steadier nerves than they'd thought. Now he was trying to play for higher stakes than he could afford, though. Really, he couldn't afford anything. None of them could. Not even Sokolov, even though he was happy to play the role of big boss man. He was on just as tight a leash as the rest of them. A noose around the neck was still a noose even if it was encrusted with diamonds.

Maybe the Finn hadn't cared as much about the woman as they had thought. Maybe it had all been an act. Regardless, kidnapping his daughter was sure to snap him out of his delusions of grandeur.

★ ★ ★

Lumikki stared at the noodles in her bowl, which were a shade somewhere between gray and beige. Elisa had been telling the truth when she said she couldn't cook. Apparently, the freezer held a supply of meals her mother had premade for her, but warming them up was "such a hassle" that Elisa preferred to eat instant ramen. Lumikki sampled the limp strands floating in salty broth and decided to power through. Or actually, the low, steady growling of her stomach decided for her.

She was insanely hungry. Morning had turned to afternoon, and Lumikki's only thought was when she was going to get home. Whenever she tried to leave, Elisa came up with some excuse why she had to stay. She really was afraid of being alone.

Their conversation was going nowhere. They had gone over everything related to the money. They had debated whether it was meant for the man in the leather coat next door. Elisa was convinced it must be.

"My mom and dad couldn't be mixed up in anything this weird. They're good people."

Nonetheless, Lumikki knew they couldn't rule out the possibility that the money was meant for one of Elisa's parents. So she'd asked what Elisa's mother did for work. Apparently, she worked for a cosmetics company as part of a team that handled their international business. Not a top executive or anything, but Elisa said she earned a fair amount.

"She spends almost half the time traveling," Elisa said, gazing out the window.

Lumikki saw a mixture of irritation and wistfulness in her face.

"Luckily, Dad is almost always home," Elisa continued, smiling. "Except, of course, this last weekend."

Elisa's dad, the police officer.

"What kind of policeman is your father?" Lumikki asked.

Elisa hung her head, mortified. "Narcotics," she replied.

The old saying about the shoemaker's children going barefoot and all that. Lumikki would have been amused if she hadn't been so irritated by Elisa's stupidity. A narcotics officer's daughter messing around with illegal drugs. You'd think Elisa wouldn't have any reason to take risks like that. Lumikki didn't say anything, but Elisa interpreted her silence correctly.

"Come on, I only use sometimes, and it's just recreational!" she said defensively. "I'm not a junkie or anything. I know my limits. And I already said that I'm never going to use again. I'm straight edge from now on."

"You could probably ask your dad sometime how many 'recreational users' in this city have completely messed up their lives. But I didn't come here to lecture you about your drug habit. I'm just here because I said I would help you."

"I can't talk to Daddy about the money, though, in case he does have something shady going on," Elisa said, sighing for the tenth time. "Which, of course, I don't believe. But if he did, then I couldn't trust him. He could lie to me just as easily as anyone else. And I can't go to any other police officers because he's my dad. Even if he is mixed up in something, I can't betray him. And what if he's doing some undercover operation? My head hurts!"

"What time does he come home today?" Lumikki asked.

"In a couple of hours."

"Was he acting normal yesterday?"

"I think so. But I was so focused on hiding the fact that I had that party here—and the elephant-sized secret in the back of my closet—I probably wouldn't have noticed if he was dancing the polka wearing Mickey Mouse ears."

"Pay attention. Talk to him. Don't ask anything directly, but see if you can tell what his expressions and gestures reveal. People say an awful lot without ever opening their mouths," Lumikki said. "And keep an eye on that neighbor. If the money was meant for him, he's sure to start acting even weirder since he didn't get it."

Elisa looked at her like a child grateful an adult had stepped in to handle things. She stood up from the table, and walked over. "Thanks," she said, hugging her quickly.

To Lumikki's astonishment, it didn't feel so unpleasant this time. Elisa returned to her chair and continued eating her noodles, sucking in her cheeks as she slurped them up and then drinking the broth from the bowl. She looked like a little girl.

"I'll talk to Daddy. And spy on that neighbor. Maybe I'll find some perfectly logical explanation for all of this. And then I can think about what to do with the money. Tuukka and Kasper aren't going to like giving theirs up, but I can get them to fall in line if I want to," Elisa said, and smiled.

Something about her sudden self-confidence was touching.

"Are you still afraid?" Lumikki asked.

"Not nearly so much."

"Okay. Then I'm going home."

Elisa tried a disappointed puppy dog expression, but Lumikki stood firm. That was enough playing girlfriend for today. She had already gone above and beyond.

Lumikki pulled on her coat, laced her combat boots up tight, and wrapped her scarf around her neck. She reached for her mittens on the hat shelf and then groped for her knit cap, which had slid farther back. She had to stand up on her tiptoes to get a grip on the edge of it. Yanking, she heard an ominous sound.

"Shoot!" Elisa exclaimed as Lumikki pulled down her half-unraveled hat. "There's a nail up there from some hooks we never hung right. I've ripped a couple of things on it too."

"It's fine. I can wrap my scarf around my ears," Lumikki said.

"No, here, take one of mine," Elisa said, already pulling a red wool hat down over Lumikki's head.

"Great. Okay. Thanks."

Lumikki stood in the hall for a few more seconds. She felt like there was something else encouraging she was supposed to say.

"Take care," she finally said when she couldn't come up with anything else. She didn't have much practice with offering comfort to others in distress.

"You too," Elisa said. "If you want, you can go out through the back. Those front steps get really slippery."

She was biting her lip, looking like she wanted to say something more but didn't. Lumikki didn't ask what the threesome was going to do next. She had a bad feeling this wouldn't be her last visit to Elisa's house.

Coming had been a mistake.

9

Boris Sokolov answered his cell phone before it could make it through the first bar of "You Only Live Twice."

"Well?"

"She just left through the back. Coming up the hill now," Viivo Tamm said.

Sokolov nodded quickly to the Estonian sitting beside him, who started the van.

"Are you sure it's the right girl?" Boris asked.

"Yes. Same red hat as before," Viivo replied.

"When you see us get close enough, run at her. Don't say anything. We have to get her on the first try," Boris said, and hung up.

He rubbed his frozen hands together to warm them up. They had to grab the girl and get her into the back of the van instantly. No one could see. And the less the girl saw, the better. And they shouldn't be too rough. She had to remain unharmed. A couple of bruises wouldn't hurt, of course. She had to know they were serious.

Because they were. In a slightly different way than she would think, though.

Once they had her, they would send a video to her dear daddy's cell phone. That would bring him to his senses. He would regret trying to play with the big boys. Boris hoped so, anyway. That he would promise to play nice from now on. Agree to forgo his next payment as a gesture of goodwill. Swear to do everything they asked.

That would be enough.

Then they would let the girl out of the van and drive off to get the decals and license plate switched. That was a big investment for one intimidation job, but in this case, it would be worth the cost. Boris Sokolov had instructions from higher up, and they had promised to cover all the expenses with a little extra thrown in. They couldn't afford to lose their inside man. But even more than that, he couldn't afford to lose them.

Of course, the girl would run home to tell Daddy that big bad men had kidnapped her. Her father would act surprised, asking for details and descriptions, promising to file a police report and catch the bastards.

No, he'd say, she wouldn't have to give any statement at the police station. Telling Daddy was enough. Daddy knew how traumatic an experience like that could be, and he didn't want to torment his daughter with an interrogation at the hands of strangers.

Boris almost laughed, imagining the man struggling to suppress his rage. How he wouldn't be able to tell anyone.

But he had made his bed, and now he had to lie in it.

★ ★ ★

In spite of the cold, Lumikki decided to take the long way home over the hill. She had to shake off the headache that Elisa's perfume and asking so many questions had left her with. That the hat Elisa had lent her seemed to be marinated in the same cloying scent didn't help the situation, but the alternative would have been frostbitten ears.

She remembered how, just after moving to Tampere a year and a half earlier, she'd come to run on Pyynikki Hill for the first time. High on her newfound freedom, she'd sprinted up the whole long, exhausting incline to the observation tower as fast as she could. At the top, her legs were shaking, and the smell of the fresh doughnuts they sold at the tower had screamed that she should just relax and call it a day. Why not sit down for some coffee and a sugar-coated treat? Lumikki resisted, though, continuing her run down past the tower, letting her sneakers fall lightly on the path. The shaking subsided, and the joy of running returned.

The road took her back up a little, and then an unbelievable view of Lake Pyhäjärvi opened up to the left. Far off behind the old red brick Pyynikki Tricot factory buildings, the low August sun caressed the water to the south. As she veered off the jogging path to the cliffs to take in the view, the green smells of late summer surrounded her. Gazing at the lake, Jalkasaari Island, and the wooded suburbs of Tampere visible on the far shore, she felt completely happy for the first time in a long time. Her own life started now. Freedom started now.

Today, freedom and happiness were a distant memory.

Lumikki tried not to think. Her thoughts just went in circles. No solution, no way out.

Or actually, there was one solution. The obvious, simple one. Go tell the police everything. Regardless of the trouble it might cause for Elisa. Or her family. That wasn't her problem. But now Elisa trusted her. And Lumikki knew she couldn't betray that trust. Too many people had done that to her. Dead end.

Lumikki started walking up the road leading to the observation tower. Clouds obscured the sun. The light dimmed. The frosted white limbs of the trees crisscrossed in every direction. This forested hillside was straight out of the pages of a charming fairy tale, but the shadows seemed like they might harbor the scariest creatures from those stories too. Freakish beings that fed on fear who snuck up behind you and pulled you into the snow, down to a cold, silent death. Or worse, turned you into a living statue of ice, unable to move or speak. Eternally living. Eternally dead.

Lumikki's breath steamed as she tried to exhale her thoughts, to empty her mind so new ideas could form. And she was finally getting there when she realized someone was following her again. She didn't need to glance back to know that she was right.

But she looked anyway. The man walking behind her had pulled his knit hat down low and hiked up his scarf to cover his mouth and nose. Behind the man was a van, which was pulling level with him.

Lumikki didn't think. She just ran. Behind her, she heard the driver downshift, and the van sped up.

The frigid air tore at her lungs, and the soles of her combat boots slipped on the icy road. Lumikki managed to glance back and get a glimpse of two men sitting in the van. They had also covered their faces, revealing only the eyes. Same gang.

No one was ahead of her. No one was to the sides. If she screamed, no one would hear.

Lumikki ran faster than she ever had in her life. The man on foot fell behind, but the van caught up to her in seconds. The door opened, and someone inside reached for Lumikki, managing to grab hold of something. Lumikki heard a ripping sound as the safety pin attaching her reflector to her coat sleeve tore a piece of fabric as it was pulled away. Lumikki threw herself to the side, made a quick turn, and plunged off the road into the forest.

Jumping over rocks and mounds of snow, she wove between the trees, ignoring the branches that scratched her face. She heard the van's brakes squeal. She heard the men charge after her. She heard the shouts, which she guessed were Russian. She knew that the confusion her abrupt turn had caused would last only so long. Lumikki knew that if they managed to surround her, she wouldn't stand a chance. She couldn't believe she could run so fast. She was in survival mode, but still she had a few seconds' head start. She had to use it right.

She wasn't going to get another chance.

Viivo Tamm swore as his leg once again sank into the snow. The girl seemed to know how to avoid the deepest drifts. Luckily, her tracks showed where she had gone, even though he lost sight of her occasionally.

"Get her!" Boris yelled from farther behind.

Get her yourself, fatso, Viivo would have liked to say. He sped up. The warmth was beginning to return to his muscles, and their ability to accept instructions was improving with every step. He was going to catch the little bitch. *You can run, but you can't hide. Running in the snow is going to start wearing you down too.* Viivo might not have been the fastest, but he had endurance.

He couldn't see the girl. The tracks led out of the thicket onto a lighted walking path. She probably hoped that some random jogger would happen along and save her. Not a chance. No one in their right mind went out for a jog in temperatures like this. Viivo glanced left and right.

The girl was gone. Fucking hell.

Then he saw something red farther down the path. The girl's hat.

It had fallen off, left behind like a signpost. Poor Little Red Riding Hood. Leaving such clear signs for the Big Bad Wolf wasn't a good idea. Boris and Linnart came stumbling out of the forest. Viivo was already running in the direction indicated by the hat, and he yelled for them to follow. The girl couldn't be far off.

Lumikki watched from a tree limb, pressed against the trunk, as the three men ran in the wrong direction. She had run onto the path, leapt into the tree leaving as few marks in the snow as possible, and shimmied up. Then she had hurled the hat as far as she could down the path.

It had worked. But it wouldn't fool them for long.

Ignoring the painful jolt to the soles of her feet as she dropped to the ground, she took off running again. Now the frozen air savaged her ears along with her lungs. But she barely felt it.

Away. Escape. Back to the road where the van stood parked. The side said MÄKINEN HVAC. Lumikki would have bet anything that none of the men were named Mäkinen. She memorized the plate number, even though she suspected it wouldn't be any use.

Her heart was pounding in her ears.

Off the hill, back onto Pyynikki Road. Now she started seeing cars and people. The lights of an approaching bus were the most beautiful thing she had ever seen. Lumikki hailed the bus from a distance, and the driver took pity on her running in the cold and pulled over before the stop. Panting, Lumikki climbed on, paid her fare, and collapsed into the nearest free seat.

Her legs were trembling. Breathing hurt. As warm air flowed into her cold-punished lungs, an uncontrollable coughing fit racked her body.

The old lady sitting across the aisle gave her a simultaneously sympathetic and disapproving look.

"You should think about wearing some sort of hat in weather like this, young lady," she said condescendingly. "Otherwise, you'll catch your death."

Lumikki coughed in reply. Feeling began to return to her ears as a tingling itch. She pressed her hands to her ears to transfer body heat from her palms. What the hell had just happened? Why had someone tried to kidnap her? If it had been an attempted rape, it seemed strange that the men would continue pursuing her so manically. They had to have some connection to the money. But why had they been after Lumikki, who was little more than a random, unlucky by-stander?

Her face still frozen in her fingers, Lumikki cursed losing the hat.

The hat. The red hat. In a flash, Lumikki realized that the men hadn't been chasing her at all. They had been chas-ing a girl in a red hat. They wanted Elisa. That made much more sense. But that meant there was no longer any doubt the money was thrown in the right yard.

Lumikki considered what would have happened if Elisa had left the house wearing the red hat instead of her. Under-standing hit her in the gut. Elisa would never have gotten away. Elisa would be in that van right now, helpless, a prisoner at the mercy of her hunters. Lumikki quickly pulled out her cell phone and texted Elisa.

Whatever you do, don't leave the house. Keep the doors locked. Don't let anyone in you don't know.

WEDNESDAY, MARCH 2

Once upon a time, there was a girl who was not afraid.

The girl ran as people run who do not fear falling. Her small, strong, nimble feet sped over the rocks and stumps. On the soles of her feet, she felt the soft moss, the sun-warmed sand, the prickly pine needles, the dewy grass. She trusted that her legs would carry her wherever she wished to go.

The girl laughed as those laugh who have not yet known humiliation. Her laughter started deep in her belly. It filled her chest, gurgled in her throat, and bubbled on her tongue. Finally, it wriggled out of her mouth, shot through the air, and burst into apple blossoms on the trees. Her laughter warmed and brightened all that surrounded her. Often it ended in hiccuping, but that did not matter because the hiccuping only made her laugh all the more.

The girl trusted as those trust for whom the earth has never given way, whom no one has ever betrayed. She hung upside down and trusted that she would not fall. Or if she fell, someone would catch her before she hit the ground.

Once upon a time, there was a girl who learned to fear.

Fairy tales do not begin this way. Other, darker stories do.

10

LUMIKKI WAS LITTLE AGAIN. SHE WAS NINE YEARS OLD. OR TEN. Or twelve. In that hell, the years ran together, sliding forward interlocked as one black indeterminate mass. Distinguishing or remembering what had happened when was impossible. What was real and what was nightmare.

But one thing she did know. She had never been afraid without good reason.

Lumikki curled herself up as small as possible and listened. She knew how to squeeze into an incredibly small space. She fit in cabinets. She fit in the dark, cluttered corners of closets. She fit into flat spaces where no one ever thought to look. She knew how to be so quiet that normal breathing sounded like a buzz saw in comparison.

Her nose ran. She let it run, controlling the overwhelming urge to sniff or wipe it with her sleeve. Thin, watery snot ran onto her lips. She did not lick. The mucus continued down to her jaw and then dripped onto her knee. It had no significance. Her jeans were already dirty anyway. Mom would wonder about it at home. Mom would wonder, and she would keep her mouth shut tight.

There were things best not talked about.

There were things that only got worse if you named them out loud.

Lumikki listened. She heard the steps as they approached. She concentrated on them in order to stay calm. If she gave power to the fear, staying quiet would be impossible. She closed her eyes and thought of untouched, freshly fallen snow. She imagined the blue twilight. She made a rabbit bound across the snow, leaving beautiful, uniform tracks. Two small circles, one in front of the other, then two oblong marks side by side. The tracks calmed her nerves.

Nothing bad could happen once the rabbit had run safely across the snow.

Nothing bad could happen with the first stars appearing in the sky.

Nothing bad could happen with Grandmother's snug cottage just a few steps away and the porch light burning brightly.

Lumikki listened as the steps retreated. She breathed a little more freely.

She had succeeded in staying hidden. She had not been found out.

What would it feel like not to need to be afraid every day?

★　★　★

Lumikki did not wake up with a start. She shifted gradually from sleeping to wakefulness, feeling her legs and arms growing longer, her body changing from a girl's to a woman's, uncoiling from a ball. She accepted the years that separated her from the Lumikki of her dreams. She was not small anymore. She was seventeen. And she hadn't needed to be afraid every day for a long time now.

Except she was again. Because she had gone and meddled in someone else's affairs.

Elisa had been calling her all night, hysterical, jumping at every squeak and groan of the cold house, wanting to hear Lumikki's reassuring voice. She had panicked when her father didn't come home when he said he would. In the middle of one call, Elisa suddenly shrieked. Lumikki listened as Elisa ran somewhere, slammed a door behind her, and turned a lock.

"Someone just came in downstairs," Elisa croaked into the phone.

"Okay. Where are you now?"

"I locked myself in the bathroom."

Lumikki had surmised as much from the sounds. Apparently, Elisa did not know how to move silently. She had never needed to learn. If a professional killer had forced his way into the house, the noise she was making would lead him to her instantly. And besides, a locked bathroom was probably the worst possible hiding place. She would be like a microwavable TV dinner in there. All you had to do was use enough force to open the packaging and then devour the contents. You didn't even really have to heat it up.

"Did whoever it is break down the door?" Lumikki had asked.

"No, they used a key."

Lumikki had felt like hanging up right then and there instead of waiting for Elisa's next sentence, which was beyond predictable even before she opened her mouth.

"Huh. Maybe it's my dad. Yeah, he's calling me from downstairs," Elisa had whispered into the phone.

No shit, Sherlock.

"Good. I'm hanging up now," Lumikki had said firmly.

"Don't go! Or, I mean, not before you promise to come back tomorrow. I can't be here alone, and I can't go out." Elisa's voice had a surprising strength.

Lumikki had wanted to refuse. She had wanted to be done with the whole mess while it was still possible to get out. Her pursuers hadn't gotten a good look at her. She could still wash her hands of this. They weren't really even dirty yet. She wasn't the one who dove into a bag of bloody money with both hands.

Lumikki felt like banging her head against the wall after ending the call. She had promised Elisa she'd come. Why had she done that? Again.

Boris Sokolov drummed his fingers against the side of his beer glass. The beer was flat and foul-tasting. An excellent fit for his mood. The first beer-hungry bar maggots had crawled out of their holes and were already sitting in the dimly lit room at their regular tables. Boris had reserved a booth for himself and the Estonians. By all appearances, no one had bothered to wipe down the table at the end of last night's shift. And why should they bother? That fit his mood perfectly too.

They had botched it. Pulled a Russki, the Finns sitting at their usual tables would have said, and this time, Boris wouldn't have been able to argue. They had to abandon the kidnapping plan. They'd had one chance, and they'd wasted it. Boris had received a short text message simply saying that he needed to handle the job. He was personally responsible.

He had to come up with some other way to scare this guy back into line.

"What if he doesn't realize Natalia is dead?" Viivo Tamm suggested, following the question with a long pull from his glass.

"He has to know. Who else's blood would he think was on the money?" Boris asked.

Viivo shrugged. Linnart Kask said nothing. Sometimes Boris suspected that Linnart was even simpler than he let on.

Boris considered Viivo's words. Could there be something to that? What if the cop really didn't understand that his beloved Natalia was a corpse? Natalia might not have told him about her plan to escape with the money. Right now, the cop might just be irritated that he had to deal with a bunch of stained cash. Maybe that was why he was claiming he hadn't received it at all.

Boris had thought the cop and Natalia genuinely cared about each other. He had been certain that they'd planned her getaway together. Perhaps he had underestimated Natalia's ability to make her own decisions. Natalia might have finally realized that it didn't pay to trust anyone too much and that no one was going to save her. On some level, Boris understood Natalia's decision.

He had never said it to Natalia, but at times, he had thought of her as the daughter he never had. A small part of Boris would have liked to let Natalia escape. But a larger part of him had understood the world of trouble he would have brought on himself if he had. That was why he'd had to harden his heart and think of Natalia running across the snow as a rabbit, a pest and a nuisance. Only then was he able to pull the trigger.

But even if the cop hadn't known about Natalia's plan, that didn't fix their current problem. That he was trying to shake them down. That they had to put a stop to it, and fast.

Browsing the calendar on his phone was Boris's way of trying to calm his nerves. Usually it worked. Now it gave him an idea.

"I think Natalia is going to send our policeman an invitation to a party soon," he said with a smile.

The Estonians looked at him in astonishment. *Boneheads.* Boris felt like he had the only brain in their troika. Luckily, it was a good one. Leaving the rest of the swill in his glass, he went to the bar to order a double whiskey. He had earned it.

Lumikki almost turned around and walked out when she saw the two extra pairs of shoes by the door. Men's sizes 9 and 11. She didn't remember agreeing to come to any Huey, Dewey, and Louie club meeting.

"Let's go over what exactly I'm doing here one more

time, since apparently Tuukka and Kasper are here too," Lumikki said to Elisa, who stared at her feet in embarrassment.

Feet wearing pink-and-black striped socks, of course.

"Well, see . . . you're the only one who knows how to fix this. Since you're so smart," Elisa said.

The bootlicking, unctuous voice and accompanying sickly sweet smile backfired. Lumikki started pulling her combat boots back on.

"I only came because you were scared and alone. No, because you demanded that I come. Because you can't deal with being alone. Well, you clearly aren't alone anymore. Problem solved. So I can go."

Elisa slipped between Lumikki and the door.

"You can't go now. Tuukka and Kasper forced their way in after they realized I wasn't at school. They didn't believe me when I said I had a migraine. I can't get through this without you," Elisa pleaded.

Lumikki's fingers fiddled with her bootlaces for a few seconds.

She'd promised herself she wasn't going to be afraid anymore. She'd only been thinking of herself then, though. She hadn't realized that she could be afraid for someone else. If she left now and closed the door behind her, she might get herself out of all of this. She wouldn't be getting away from the fear, though. She could ignore Elisa's calls and text messages. She could even get an unlisted number. She could avoid seeing Elisa at school. She could treat her like she was invisible.

But she couldn't stop herself from thinking. She couldn't stop herself from contemplating what could happen to Elisa and whether the men who'd chased Lumikki might get their hands on her eventually. She would be afraid on Elisa's behalf. She didn't want that.

Lumikki knew she was already in too deep, in over her combat boots. It was all the same now whether she sank in up to her knees or her waist or her neck.

In hot water. Up shit creek. Not free. Lumikki hated that. But she couldn't do anything about it.

Sighing deeply, she began pulling off her boots.

"I'll stay. But just so you know, if Tuukka tries his tough-guy routine again, I'm calling the police that very second and throwing you all to the wolves."

Elisa clapped her hands enthusiastically. Lumikki might as well have been listening to her own death knell.

11

"DID YOU FIND ANYTHING OUT FROM YOUR DAD LAST NIGHT?" Tuukka asked Elisa as she brought them large glasses of Coke in the living room.

Kasper had asked for his with a kick, but Elisa's expression wiped the grin off his face.

Lumikki glanced at Tuukka. *Elisa must have told the boys everything. Blabbermouth.* But maybe it was best this way. Talking would be easier if they were all looking at the same map.

"My brain was barely functioning, I was so hysterical about those men chasing Lumikki. I mean, chasing her thinking she was me. In the state I was in, I was lucky I could keep my mouth shut, let alone pull off some sort of cunning secret interrogation."

Elisa set down the serving tray with the Coke glasses on the living room table. Ice cubes clinked against each other. She looked even more tired than she had the day before.

The circles under her eyes were darker, her hair hadn't been washed, and she didn't have any makeup on. She was like a smudge on the pure linen fabric of the stylish living room, a stain on the furnishings that oozed high design. From the ceiling hung a large bulbous lamp made of thin strips of wood laminate. Scandinavian lines, artless elegance, all for a price.

Lumikki found herself wondering again how they could pay for all of this on the salaries of a police officer and a cosmetics sales agent. No one on the police force was making bank, and Elisa's mom's salary couldn't be that amazing either. An inheritance? Possible.

Or maybe it had something to do with a trash bag full of bloody money.

"Okay. So then let's check your mom and dad's computers," Kasper said with the self-assurance of an up-and-coming small-time hood.

"Mom took her laptop with her on her trip, but Dad's computer is in his office over there. But I don't know—"

Kasper was already marching to the office door before Elisa could complete her sentence. "I'll check the computer. You guys check the files and stuff," Kasper said.

Lumikki, Tuukka, and Elisa followed him into the office.

"Isn't this sort of illegal?" Elisa asked as she riffled through her father's desk drawers.

"I don't remember legality being much of an obstacle for you before," Tuukka said with a laugh.

Elisa sighed. "Maybe it should be."

Lumikki agreed, but she didn't say so. Instead, she voiced another concern.

"We aren't going to find anything about your dad's work here. He's got to have super strict rules about what papers he can bring home. Probably none. And the computer is a home computer. All of his work stuff is going to be on his work computer."

"You're right. Why didn't I remember that?"

"Let's look anyway," Tuukka insisted. "There's no way he would store anything at the police station about crimes he's committing. That place is crawling with snitches."

Elisa's scowl limited Tuukka's smile to the faint curl at the corner of his mouth. They searched in silence, without results. The office didn't reveal anything but a meticulous father who kept his tax returns, insurance policies, and bills organized, and the folders on his computer clean.

"He hasn't even been looking at any porn sites," Kasper grumbled impatiently.

"Gross! Of course he hasn't." Elisa shuddered.

"But you have," Tuukka snickered. "I've done enough snooping around your computer to know that."

"Once, maybe, when a friend sent a link, and I clicked on it without thinking," Elisa insisted.

Lumikki couldn't stand listening to the trio's pointless blather. What irritated her the most was Elisa's voice, which around the boys had turned mousy, and her comments, which were growing increasingly stupid. Lumikki knew the phenomenon. All through middle school, she had watched in bewilderment as it took hold. After the summer between sixth and seventh grade, some of the girls came back to school acting like they'd dropped half of their brains in a lake somewhere. Girls who used to be really smart suddenly couldn't even do simple math or run a hundred-yard dash without complaining that they were "gonna die."

"Seriously, I'm gonna die!" they would squeal over and over throughout the day, sometimes thrilled, sometimes feigning helplessness. They painted their eyes and snapped bubble gum. It had taken Lumikki some time to figure out that the girls' stupid act was meant for the boys. That their pathetic behavior was a signal that they were small, cute, and harmless. And sexy in just the right way for certain boys.

They shrank and dumbed themselves down so the best-looking boys in class could feel smarter and stronger. Lumikki had always wondered why the boys couldn't see through the act. Didn't they find it humiliating that the girls thought they had to pretend so the boys could feel superior? Of course, some boys did see through it, but the show wasn't for their benefit anyway. They were too smart to be sexy.

For some reason, intelligence wasn't sexy in middle school. If you wanted to be sexy, you had to avoid intelligence like the plague. Smart meant the same thing as boring, annoying, irritating, and, if not actually ugly, at least nothing much to look at.

Lumikki had thought things would change after middle school. Partly they did, but partly not. Now she could see that even some really accomplished adult women dumbed themselves down in male company. It was embarrassing to watch. She hoped Elisa had one foot still stuck in junior high and her behavior was a result of that, rather than some deeper issue or ingrained pattern.

"Let me take a look at the computer for a sec too," Lumikki said to Kasper.

The boy looked at her dubiously.

"There isn't anything there," Kasper said.

"Just let me look anyway," Lumikki insisted calmly. "Sometimes there's a lot more on a machine than it seems on the surface."

"Ooh, so our super detective is also some kind of fucking computer genius," Tuukka said mockingly.

"Yeah. I'm the secret love child of Hercule Poirot and Lisbeth Salander," Lumikki replied without the slightest wavering in her expression, and sat down in the rolling chair Kasper had just vacated dramatically.

The trio stood behind her, watching. Lumikki hated that.

"So you're Lumikki Poisander then?" Kasper asked, trying to keep up the joke.

No one laughed.

"Lumikki . . . Lumikki."

Kasper seemed to be savoring the name, drawing out each syllable.

"You must have a nickname," he said finally.

"No, I don't," Lumikki replied without turning around.

"Lumi?"

"No."

"Mikki?"

"You think?"

"Okay, maybe not. What about Snow White, then? That is your—"

Lumikki pushed the chair back so suddenly that it banged into Kasper, and she spun around.

"Ouch! Watch it." Kasper massaged his knee irritably.

"Chill. Out. This could take a while," Lumikki said, throwing Elisa a meaningful look.

Fortunately, the girl still knew how to use her brain some-times. "Let's go finish our Cokes in the living room," Elisa said. "Shout if you find anything."

Lumikki nodded and turned back to the monitor. After a moment, she heard the door close behind her. Blessed quiet.

She had to act quickly. No way would the quiet last.

12

TERHO VÄISÄNEN TURNED UP HIS COLLAR AND PULLED THE green scarf his daughter had knitted him over his mouth. The cold sank its sharp claws into any bare patch of skin as soon as he stepped outside. He considered driving home from the police station to Pyynikki in his car, but he decided to walk after all. Maybe the cold would stimulate his brain, which had been unacceptably sluggish.

Two questions were bothering Terho.

Where was his money?

Where was Natalia?

And was that the order of importance of those questions? Of course not, but sometimes Natalia went quiet for several days, sometimes even weeks. She didn't always have time to answer Terho's calls and texts and emails. He was used to that. So Natalia's disappearance didn't really mean anything yet. In contrast, it definitely did mean something that Boris Sokolov had practically reached through the cell phone to throttle Terho when he called to ask about the money. Sokolov said the money had already been delivered.

But it hadn't.

Either Sokolov was lying, or the Estonians were lying to Sokolov. The latter was more likely. Terho had actually been surprised that they had gone so long without one of them trying to stick his hand in the cookie jar and make some quick cash. He chalked this discipline up to the Estonians having seen how Sokolov dealt with disloyalty. No one wanted to experience Sokolov's brand of justice. And of course, Sokolov took his orders from higher up just like everyone else. The hierarchy of power and fear kept everyone in line.

But now someone had decided to take a little extra for himself.

Terho hated the thought that a system that had worked so well might be unraveling. He had done his own part without asking any questions. From the beginning, he was in this for the money, and he still needed it. If the cash stopped coming, his options would be limited. He hadn't built himself a safety net for the future, even though he knew he should have. The amount he had in savings was pathetic. Of course, he could always burn Sokolov and company in revenge, but that was impossible without implicating himself with them. All that would be left was smoking wreckage.

He couldn't let that happen.

Because negotiations hadn't gone anywhere with Sokolov, he would have to try making an agreement directly with Polar Bear. That wouldn't be easy. Polar Bear wrote his own rules, and if he didn't like the way the game was going, he simply knocked the other players off the board.

Terho walked along the Tampere Highway and cursed himself for getting involved. Not only was it criminal, but it was morally wrong. No matter how many mornings he had spent staring out the window while his family still slept, rationalizing how the arrangement had its good sides. For the police force and for the community. He had received information from Sokolov that had helped the police capture any number of dealers and traffickers. They had cleaned up the Tampere underworld so thoroughly that Terho's unit had received commendations from the highest levels of government. Terho reminded himself of that as he watched the neighboring homes waking from their morning slumber. The slowly rising sun mocked his self-deception, though. He had to avert his gaze from the sun, pour more milk in his coffee, and look elsewhere as he continued lying to himself.

Back then, years ago, taking the offer had seemed like the only viable option. Gambling debts and unpaid loans hung around his neck. Terho had drifted imperceptibly into a downward spiral of gambling. At first, it had been an easy way to relax and clear his head after a hard day at work, but little by little, it became a full-blown addiction. Playing online was far too easy, and he had to play for money so it would feel like something—so he could get the adrenaline rush he needed. He also had a wife at home with expensive tastes, and at that point, Terho still wanted to give her all the best the world could offer.

And then there was Elisa, his daughter, whom he loved more than he had ever thought possible. Everything he had done had also been for her. So she would never have to be ashamed of her house or her clothes. Or ever worry about money. Too often as a child and teenager, Terho had been forced to lie and say a pair of flea-market jeans was actually new, or that a coat from his cousin was really from a trip they took abroad. The truth was that his father drank up their middle-class income. Terho had been so ashamed that he'd sworn off alcohol and joined the narcotics police, where at least he could fight against illegal drugs, since there was nothing he could do about the deadly drug called alcohol.

Nevertheless, a predisposition to addiction had been passed from father to son. The need to get kicks from something, fast and without a lot of thought. But Terho had always made sure his gambling didn't interfere with his family. It was his private, personal vice. He had even succeeded in cutting down how much he played compared to his worst addict years, but that didn't mean he could manage without a regular fix.

For the past year, there'd been an additional reason for Terho to cooperate with Sokolov—Natalia. Despite how much younger she was, he was helplessly in love, head over heels like a teenager. He'd known from the beginning that it was crazy and hopeless and dangerous, but he couldn't resist Natalia's smile and those big, innocent eyes that you'd never guess had seen so much. He was already mourning the fact that, at some point, he would be forced to give up Natalia's company, her silky smooth skin, and the dimples in her cheeks. It was unavoidable. The relationship couldn't go on forever unless Terho was willing to sacrifice his marriage, his family, and ultimately his career. He wasn't ready for that, despite having promised her in tender moments that he would leave his wife and begin a new life with her. The promises of a man in love, promises that he could never keep. Natalia understood, he told himself. She was a smart young woman, smarter than she seemed.

But Terho wanted to save her. He owed her at least that much. He wanted Natalia to have a better life and not have to work for Sokolov anymore. Terho didn't know how he would handle it yet, but he was sure he'd figure something out. That was another reason the whole arrangement couldn't fall apart just because the Estonians couldn't keep their paws out of the piggy bank.

In the park, a painfully cold wind was coming in off the lake, making Terho regret not driving. Even his high-tech down coat was no match for this insanely cold winter.

A work meeting had been canceled at the last minute, leaving him with a good hour of free time. He'd decided to use it to stop by home and make lunch for himself and Elisa, who was suffering from a migraine or some kind of female issue. Or plain old laziness. Terho had to admit it to himself. His daughter was sweet and popular and the dearest thing to him in the world, but she wasn't the brightest bulb on the Christmas tree. Maybe a magnet school wasn't really the place for her after all.

Terho went over his plan.

He would have to contact Polar Bear. The only way to do that would be via email, and he'd have to send it from his home computer, because he didn't dare send it from work or from his phone.

At the same time, he'd write to Natalia again and ask why he hadn't heard from her. He missed her so much. The longing chilled his bones even more than the biting wind.

★ ★ ★

Brown eyes. Bleached hair with just a hint of darker roots. Here and there, streaks lighter than the rest. Hair extensions. Heavily plucked eyebrows. Lips that might be enhanced or might just be that full naturally.

Age: somewhere between seventeen and twenty-five?

In most of her pictures, she struck a serious pose, lips slightly parted. In one picture, though, she was smiling, showing off deep dimples. The smile made her look younger and more vulnerable. In the same picture was a middle-aged man who had exactly the same nose as Elisa. The woman wore expensive clothing that announced how expensive it was. There was one more close-up of the couple, which they'd probably taken themselves with a camera phone, that showed them kissing and laughing. They looked obscenely happy.

Lumikki felt like a voyeur looking at the pictures, which had been hidden rather primitively on the computer. Before finding them, she had already located a username and password for an anonymous email account. The mail folders were empty, though. Elisa's dad either didn't use it or—more likely—he always deleted emails after reading them.

"Elisa," Lumikki called.

Elisa came to the door. Mercifully, Tuukka and Kasper had decided to entertain themselves by playing Wii in the living room.

"Will you close the door, please?" Lumikki asked, and Elisa complied. Then Lumikki took a deep breath and continued.

"I'm assuming the woman in these pictures isn't your mom."

13

ELISA WRAPPED HER ARMS AROUND HERSELF. SHE SUDDENLY FELT very cold. She wanted to close her eyes and not see the pictures, but even that wouldn't have helped. They were already burned deep into her brain and would be playing on an internal movie screen that night when she closed her eyes and tried to sleep.

How could Daddy do this to her? And to her mom?

Elisa wasn't stupid. For a long time, she had known her parents' relationship wasn't happy in a romantic sense and that they were mostly still together out of habit and convenience. Still, it felt inconceivable to think that Daddy had cheated on her mom. Daddy wasn't like that. Daddy was honest and honorable and dependable. Daddy was the kind of man who got divorced before starting anything new. Actually, Elisa hadn't been as sure about her mom. Elisa wouldn't have been surprised to learn that her mom didn't always spend her nights alone when she was traveling for work.

But Daddy. With a younger woman, barely older than Elisa herself. The whole idea made her sick. Even worse than the relationship was the secrecy and the lying. If it was even a real relationship. It could just be— But then why would Daddy have kept the pictures on his computer? They had to mean something because he wanted to be able to look at them again.

"Maybe . . ."

Elisa heard Lumikki's voice as if in a dream. What if this was all a dream and she could wake up . . . right . . . now!

The door flew open, and Tuukka and Kasper tumbled in.

"Important girl talk going on in here? Or has our computer whiz actually found something? Woo-hoo."

Lumikki felt awkward having Elisa, Kasper, and Tuukka staring over her shoulder at the pictures. The worst thing about it was being able to sense Elisa's embarrassment without even turning around.

"Maybe she's just . . . or I mean, maybe Daddy's just . . . ," Elisa said, trying desperately to articulate any sort of explanation.

"Let's face it," Kasper said. "Your dad is banging some young chick."

All of their thoughts spoken aloud. Perhaps not word for word, but the bottom line was the same.

"There could be some other explanation," Elisa said feebly.

Lumikki could hear from her voice that Elisa knew Kasper was right.

"I'd bet anything this has something to do with the money," Tuukka said. "Two secrets like this at once can't be a coincidence."

"But how?" Elisa asked.

"Doesn't she look a little bit Russian?" Kasper asked. "Maybe she's a whor—sorry, I mean, prostitute. Maybe your dad is mixed up in some kind of sex business."

Elisa shook her head. Looking at her now, Lumikki realized Elisa was on the verge of tears.

"Or maybe—" Tuukka was going to take a stab at speculating now.

But just then, the computer chimed to signal the arrival of a new email. Lumikki had left the anonymous account open just in case something of interest happened to come in.

Bull's-eye.

The sender was using an anonymous account too. The handle, "Beatifulrose," and a top-level domain name didn't reveal much. Lumikki read the message out loud. It was written in English.

My love,

    I had to create another email address. Just to be careful. Polar Bear is having a party on Friday. Wants you to be there. And so do I. There will be a black car picking you up at 8 p.m. Because the theme is fairy tales and because I know what you like, I'm going as the Snow Queen. I've got something important to tell you.

                                 Kisses, N

*P.S. Please delete this message right after reading
as always. We have to be extra careful.*

Tuukka, Kasper, and Elisa looked at each other.

"What the hell does that mean?" Elisa asked.

"Polar Bear, Polar Bear . . . ," Kasper repeated. "Oh my God. Polar Bear. Your dad just got invited to one of Polar Bear's parties."

"What? Whose party?"

"Polar Bear's!" Kasper almost yelled. "He's a legend. I mean, I don't know much more than that he's some kind of super big shot who everyone respects. I've heard he runs all kinds of different legal and illegal businesses, and basically no one has ever seen him. The rumors about his parties are totally wild. Apparently, he has some kind of crazy mansion or castle where he hosts these off-the-hook blowouts. Everybody goes. I mean, everybody who's rich and important."

"What is this Polar Bear guy's real name?" Lumikki asked.

Kasper looked at her in amusement. "How should I know? You'd have to be a serious insider to know something like that."

"So he's like a mob boss or something?" Elisa had instinctively lowered her voice.

Kasper spread his arms.

"Well, I doubt he'd want the cops to know about all his businesses. I mean, what do I know? But he's so rich and crafty that he never gets caught. He never gets his own hands dirty."

"How do you know about all this?" Tuukka asked.

A satisfied smile appeared on Kasper's lips. Lumikki could

see that Kasper thought he was way slicker than the rest of them.

"I have my sources. When you spend time on the street, you hear things. And don't bother asking any more. I get you guys pills, and I get you information. That's all you need to know."

While the others were talking, Lumikki copied the email down word for word on a slip of paper and shoved it in her pants pocket.

"Be that as it may, we have to trash this email," she said. "Unfortunately, it says that it's been opened once already now, so your dad will know someone's been in his account."

Lumikki prepared to delete the message.

Terho Väisänen's fingers were frozen, even though his gloves were supposed to be Windstopper fabric with all kinds of insulating layers. He tried to warm up his joints enough to get the key into the front door lock.

He thought back on the previous December when it was only a couple of degrees below freezing, with snow falling so gently you almost didn't notice it. He had been standing with Natalia by a sculpture in Tampella. The sculpture radiated a blue light that made Natalia's face look ethereal.

They had just gone for coffee. The new housing development on the river was relatively safe. He didn't know anyone who lived there. Neither his wife nor Elisa had any reason to visit. Only people who lived in the area should be around, since it wasn't on the way to anywhere else. There weren't any special stores or restaurants that would inspire people to go out of their way. The coffee shop was just barely scraping by on the euros that local residents brought in. In Tampella, they dared to appear in public together, even though there were still risks.

Sometimes you had to take a risk. And besides, the fear of getting caught added to the thrill. Of course, Terho had a cover story in case a friend or a friend of a friend happened to see them together. He could always point to his work, intelligence gathering, the importance of confidentiality and all that. He could make them think that Natalia was giving him information, but that he couldn't reveal anything more than that. Hush-hush. Terho was relieved he hadn't had to use his cover story yet.

Natalia had forgotten her gloves. She blew on her small hands. Terho took them between his own to warm them up. She smiled. Snowflakes stuck to her hair, reflecting the blue light of the statue. Natalia was wearing a white coat and white boots. She looked more beautiful than she ever had before.

"My snow queen," Terho breathed into her ear.

Suddenly, he was filled with an intense desire to warm Natalia all over, to press his burning palms against her cool skin, to melt every flake of snow.

"Let's go," he said hoarsely, and pulled Natalia along, quickening his steps. In five minutes, they were at the reception desk of Hotel Tammer. They got a room. He made a quick call to his wife, informing her that he would be working late into the night. Then he turned back to Natalia, who didn't look so much like a fairy-tale creature anymore in the warm yellow light of the hotel room. That didn't matter, though. The mental image had already created the desire. Pulling Natalia against him, he closed his eyes.

Terho Väisänen returned to the present, clumsy fingers still fighting with his key, and uttered a string of curses.

Lumikki heard the sounds first.

In a hushed voice, she said, "Someone's coming."

Elisa jumped. "The men who chased you! The killers!"

Lumikki restrained her desire to slap her hand over Elisa's mouth. Did she really have such an underdeveloped sense of self-preservation? Did living in a pink-and-black room pickle your brain and turn your thoughts to mush?

"Let's just stay calm and keep quiet. Obviously, whoever it is has a key. I'm guessing it's your dad. The important thing is that we don't let him know we were in here by making too much noise."

As she spoke, Lumikki calmly deleted the email, logged out of the account, closed the secret picture folder and browser window, and turned off the machine. To Lumikki, it felt like each step took an agonizingly long time. In reality, of course, it all happened in a matter of seconds.

Then again, it also only took a few seconds for the person at the door to get the key into the lock and click it open.

"Go upstairs."

Lumikki issued her command as quietly as possible. It was enough to convince Elisa, Tuukka, and Kasper, who slipped out of the study and rushed to the stairs. They probably thought they were being quiet, but to Lumikki, their exit sounded like a herd of wildebeests that had just heard a lion roar.

Turn off already. Turn off.

The computer stayed stuck at the "Shutting down ..." screen for too long. Lumikki guessed that the machine had the same problem her own laptop did, and occasionally just refused to power down for no particular reason.

She heard the door open. Fortunately, the front door did not have a direct line of sight to the office. Someone large stepped into the house. A man.

Lumikki controlled her breath, concentrating on keeping her heart rate in check. Then she firmly pressed the power button and held it down. The next time it booted up, the machine might complain about not being shut down properly, which could arouse Elisa's father's suspicion, but right now, taking that risk was her only option. Most likely, he would act just like anyone else and wonder for two seconds about why the machine had crashed, then shrug and start thinking about buying a new one soon.

Turn off already.

The screen went black.

"Elisa! I decided to come home for lunch! I'll make something for us," he shouted up the stairs.

Good. Lumikki had been right.

Quietly, she hid behind the office door, hoping fervently that Elisa's dad wouldn't come in there first.

She could hear him taking off his cold weather clothes. Then his steps approached the office.

Keep walking.

He was already moving past the office into the kitchen,

but then changed his mind and stepped into the room. Lumikki held her breath. She was flat. She was odorless. She did not exist.

Don't sit down. Lumikki knew that the chair would be warm.

Elisa's dad did not sit. Standing at the desk, he sorted the mail. Lumikki still held her breath. She knew she could hold her breath calmly for at least two minutes. Elisa's dad tossed a couple of envelopes, presumably bills, toward the back corner of the desk. Then he headed to the kitchen.

"What do you want? Should I make some pasta? Or maybe that curried chicken soup you like? I really need something hot after freezing my butt off outside."

Lumikki heard him open the refrigerator door.

Now. Coming out from behind the door, she took two steps to build up speed and then slid silently in her socks across the almost unnaturally smooth hardwood floor over to the stairs. Then she hurried up as quietly as a lion stalking that herd of wildebeest. She walked into Elisa's room so inconspicuously that she succeeded in startling the trio waiting inside.

"God, you almost gave me a heart attack," Elisa whispered. "Now get in the closet."

"Why?"

Lumikki didn't understand Elisa's train of thought. Tuukka and Kasper were happily sprawled on the couch without any intention of hiding.

Heavy steps approached up the stairs.

"I'll explain later," Elisa hissed, pushing Lumikki into the walk-in closet and quickly shutting the door.

"Do you have a friend over?" Elisa's dad asked from the top of the stairs.

"Yeah. Tuukka and Kasper came to keep me company," Elisa answered in an overly cheerful voice that anyone could tell was fake from a mile away.

"Weren't you supposed to have a migraine?" he asked suspiciously. "And aren't you boys supposed to be in school?"

"Oh, it just went away," Elisa said.

"Math class was canceled 'cause the teacher's sick," Tuukka answered.

Lumikki watched through a crack in the door as Elisa's dad looked over the threesome. He had short blond hair and an upper body that suggested time spent in the weight room. The closet was dark but roomy. It smelled of girl. Lumikki's closet never could have smelled like that.

She was hiding again. Trying not to be seen.

Lumikki closed her eyes.

You can't run. We'll always find you. And when we find you, we're going to kill you.

Kill.

You.

14

A MIDSUMMER POLE STRETCHING HIGH INTO THE SKY, FES-
tooned with garlands of flowers and ribbons and leaves. Balloons, balloons, and more balloons, some escaping into the
blue. The most beautiful evening of the year in the Åland
Islands, already turning to night but still as bright as day.
All of Dad's family there. The scents of summer, the distant
screeching of gulls, the twittering of the swallows. Lumikki
was wearing a white dress and a garland of dandelions
Mom made. She was singing Astrid Lindgren's "Ida's Summer Song." She didn't have a beautiful voice, and she wasn't
used to speaking Swedish in front of people, but that didn't
matter.

Cousin Emma, one year older, suddenly stood before her.
Lumikki tried to get past. She wanted to go see the midsummer pole. She wanted a balloon too, the ones Uncle Erik
was filling with helium and passing out to the kids. A red

one. Or blue. Not yellow under any circumstances. Maybe red would be best.

"Want to play?" Cousin Emma asked in Swedish. Lumikki shrugged.

"How about we play that you're my slave and you have to do everything I say?"

Lumikki shook her head.

"Well then, I could be the queen and you could be my horse."

"No," Lumikki said.

"You have to. I get to choose because we live here and I'm older."

Lumikki started to cry. "No," she said again.

Just then, Auntie Anna, Cousin Emma's mother, came up with Lumikki's mom.

"Lumikki doesn't want to play with me. She just says no to everything I suggest," Emma whined to her mother. "She isn't even close to as fun as—"

"Shh . . ." Auntie Anna stroked Emma's blond hair. "Maybe Lumikki is a little shy," she suggested. "Come on, let's go get you a balloon."

Auntie Anna took Emma by the hand. After a few steps, Emma turned back and stuck her tongue out at Lumikki. Auntie Anna and Mom didn't notice. Mom was looking out at the sea. The salty wind seemed to make her eyes water. Wiping them with the back of her hand, she sighed and, in Finnish, said to Lumikki, "It isn't good to always say no. If you say yes a little more often, you could make some friends."

Friends? Did Lumikki want friends? Did that mean she had to do whatever people wanted?

The next line of the song didn't want to come out of Lumikki's mouth anymore.

"No."

Lumikki tried to say it in a voice that precluded any further discussion on the topic.

Elisa looked at her with her big eyes. The Bambi-just-lost-his-mother look didn't work on Lumikki, though.

"But none of the rest of us can," Tuukka tried to argue. "You're the only one Elisa's dad hasn't ever seen before."

"Playing detective might have been fun in elementary school, but this isn't a game."

Lumikki opened the balcony door and let the frigid air rush into Elisa's room. She had been forced to spend nearly half an hour in the saccharine-smelling closet while Elisa and the boys enjoyed themselves downstairs eating the chicken soup her dad had made. Finally, Elisa's father had gone back to work.

Lumikki drew fresh air into her lungs. It didn't matter that it stung.

"But it might be the only way we'll ever find out what's going on," Kasper said, joining in the coaxing.

"Or maybe we should stop this fooling around and go talk to the police," Lumikki said.

No, no, no. Because of the party. Because of the drugs. Because of the break-in at the school. Because of the money. Because Elisa's dad was a cop and who was going to believe them unless they had more information, more than a few pictures and a deleted email?

"Ditching school day after day might not matter to you guys, but I'm not interested in flunking out."

Determined, Lumikki set off downstairs. Elisa, Tuukka, and Kasper followed her like puppies. All that was missing were the lolling tongues.

"All you have tomorrow is two hours of physics and two hours of PE," Elisa said. "And you're not anywhere close to missing too many classes in either of them."

Lumikki glanced at Elisa. Had she checked on her class schedule and absences? Pretty smart move. Surprisingly smart.

"If you do this one thing, I swear I won't bother you anymore." Elisa looked sincere.

Lumikki didn't give any sign that she was tempted, either by the idea that they wouldn't bother her anymore or by the actual task. She knew she would be good at it. She was good at being invisible, inconspicuous, nonexistent.

"Okay. But right now I'm going to school. I can still make art class."

Elisa's expression brightened when she realized that Lumikki had actually agreed. Spontaneously, she hugged Lumikki, who felt like a boa constrictor had her in its coils. She should have rebuffed Elisa's first surprise attack. Now she was clearly trapped in a cycle of hugging she was never going to escape.

"Thank you, thank you, thank you."

Lumikki wriggled out of the embrace. "Don't make me change my mind."

Tuukka was standing above them on the stairs, leaning on the railing and smiling crookedly. He probably thought his slanted smile was ironically sexy, but really it just looked stupid.

Outside, Lumikki looked at the clock on her phone. It was 12:35. She would have to be back here in seventeen hours.

The attacker came at Lumikki from the right. Quickly, she delivered two right jabs to his nose followed by two uppercuts to the chin. Immediately, she repeated the sequence. Two jabs, two uppercuts. Jab, jab, up, up. Lumikki's pulse was pounding around 175.

Her opponent staggered but stayed upright and continued trying to get ahold of her. Lumikki aimed her right elbow at his rib cage and then lifted up lightning fast, continuing the motion with her right fist directly into his cheek. Then she finished the job by lashing out with a quick side kick.

Her attacker lay on the ground. Sweat streamed down Lumikki's back, calves, and face.

Her attacker attempted to rise, but Lumikki firmly pushed him to the floor with her right hand.

Don't try anything, you little shit.

She started punching with her right hand, letting her fist fall with all her force on his upper body and face. At first, the blows were slow, accurate, and relentless. Little by little, their speed accelerated and they turned wild, an angry flurry of hate.

Useless to beg for mercy. This isn't church, and you're not going to be forgiven for your sins.

Salty sweat ran into Lumikki's eyes, making them sting.

She tried to blink it away but finally had to squeeze her eyes shut tight. She didn't need to see. She knew her opponent's face all too well.

You're. Never. Getting. Up. Again.

"Excellent! Now the same on the left side. You already know this combination. Go all out right from the start, everyone."

Lumikki took a couple of extra sidesteps to her sweat towel and used it to quickly dry off her eyes and forehead. Then the pounding music again filled the gym, where about forty young women, a couple of middle-aged women, and three men began moving through the same synchronized pattern of steps and strikes like parts in a finely tuned machine. This was Body Combat class.

Lumikki glanced at the large mirrors on the walls to make sure she was crouched low enough and her fists were up high enough to block her face, which was red from exertion. Diagonally behind her, a girl in a green shirt and pigtails glanced at Lumikki to copy her form. *Go right ahead and look.* Lumikki knew she was one of the best in the group. She put a hundred percent into every movement. She had the technique down.

Or the choreography, rather. Because in the end, that's all this was. A series of movements performed in time to bouncy pop songs with a dash of martial arts thrown in. Simple-enough steps for anyone to follow as they sweated their cellulite away, fighting imaginary opponents while the instructor yelled directions and encouragement. Only a couple of degrees more aggressive than aerobics.

Lumikki liked Body Combat anyway. You worked up a sweat, your muscles got toned, and getting into the right frame of mind was easy for her. She didn't want to practice a real martial art or boxing. She already knew perfectly well what it felt like to sink her fist into another person's stomach. She knew how blood erupted from a nose and how strangely warm it felt on her skin. Like half-cooled homemade jelly or jam. She didn't want a real, living target for her attacks. Two years had not made her memories of real violence any less vivid. The blue Nordic dusk of that afternoon in the school-yard was burned into her memory. Whenever it crossed her mind, she tasted acid in her mouth and smelled the sweet scent of perfume in her nose. The fragrance contained roses, vanilla, and a hint of sandalwood.

The song had changed, now something about rain falling down, but the pace remained frenetic. Lumikki didn't need rain to drench her black tank top. It was soaked through with perspiration as it was.

After class, she sat in the dressing room, allowing her breathing to level off as she unwound the wraps from her hands. In addition to supporting her wrists, they also absorbed sweat. But more than anything, they were part of the game, props for a role, a way for good little schoolgirls like her to imagine they were something else. Attitude wraps, some people called them—some in jest, some more enthusiastically.

"This new program is good. More intense than the old one."

Lumikki glanced at the person addressing her. The girl, who looked a couple of years older, was sitting at the other end of the bench, unwrapping her own wrists and clearly directing her words at Lumikki. Long red hair in a high pony-tail. Face and arms dotted with freckles. Loose black trousers and a tight black top, the same Body Combat uniform Lumikki had on. She had seen the girl in class and around the gym lots of times. And she knew the girl had seen her too. Lumikki had noticed her watching her movements. And not just her movements, but also the curve of her body, the shape of her muscles. She had sensed that the girl would talk to her at some point.

"Yeah, it's pretty good," Lumikki replied.

With a relaxed, natural motion, the redhead slid over to sit next to Lumikki. Calvin Klein One and grapefruit-scented shower gel struggled for dominance beneath the smell of her sweat. A tight biceps rounded as the girl continued removing her wrist wraps. Just at her biceps, seven freckles almost formed the constellation Gemini.

Memories forced themselves on Lumikki. There was another person who wore CK One. Who had a tattoo of Gemini on their neck. How it had felt to press her lips to the skin of that neck and place feather-soft kisses along the stars. To let her mouth linger when it reached Castor. To know that, somewhere around Pollux, the owner of the tattoo would no longer be able to resist turning, trapping Lumikki's wrists, and kissing her on the lips.

Had that really been just the summer before? It felt like a hundred years ago.

Lumikki grabbed her water bottle and took a long swig. The girl was clearly waiting for her to say something, to give some sign that moving closer had been a good idea. To take a little initiative. Lumikki saw too well where it would lead. To more conversations, more smiles, a cautious invitation to coffee, and then, inevitably, to a situation in which she would have to be cruel.

It isn't you, it's me.

Not now. Not yet. Maybe not ever.

Let's just be friends.

And both of them would know that would mean doing their best to avoid each other from that point on.

And Lumikki would never be able to explain that they were only in that situation because the girl's perfume had reminded Lumikki of someone else, and that was why they couldn't go on. She couldn't be honest. She would have to lie from the outset, and that would only lead to embarrassment, halfhearted regret, blunted vexation.

So pointless. Lumikki decided to save them both that time, to save the girl's feelings, and just continued drinking her water. The silence crossed over into awkwardness. The girl shifted uncomfortably and brushed some stray hairs back.

"Okay. See you later," she said.

Lumikki raised one hand slightly in farewell. Grabbing her gym bag, the girl moved to another spot in the dressing room so they couldn't see each other. Lumikki quietly released the air from her lungs. The euphoric feeling she'd had after Body Combat was gone. Her skimpy workout clothes were plastered cold against her skin.

The last song from class was stuck in her head—the surrender. In some things, she preferred to surrender than to fight. Sometimes that was better for everyone.

Lumikki had the sauna to herself for once. Instead of throwing water on the rocks right away, she let the warmth return to her skin, beads of sweat forming again, running from her neck down her spine. Memories from the summer and fall struggled to the surface along with the perspiration, although she tried to tell them this wasn't a good time. There was never a good time for regret and longing. Latching on to her, they clenched her stomach tight and forced her back to bend.

Light blue eyes looking straight into her own. Then quickly away. Somewhere away.

"It's better if we don't see each other anymore."

"Anymore ever?"

"At least for a little while. You get that I want to work through this alone, right? I just can't be with you right now. And it wouldn't be fair to you to make you put up with me."

Lumikki had wanted to scream. What right did anyone else have to say what the limits of her endurance were, or decide what was fair to her or not? Lumikki knew how to take care of herself. What had infuriated her was how casually she had been shut out of this other person's life and challenges. As if she was a fragile little kid who needed protecting. Lumikki had felt like hissing back that she had been through much worse and didn't need to be kept in Bubble Wrap.

She had realized that shouting wasn't going to help anything, though. Those beautiful blue eyes had made their decision. Lumikki's role was just to accept it. That was what the script said she did in this scene.

"What does 'a little while' mean? I can still call you, right?"

Lumikki had detested the high-pitched pleading in her voice. She had felt a lump of tears growing in her throat and knew she wouldn't be able to get it out. Years had passed since she'd lost the ability to cry. Last summer, she thought maybe she'd find it again, but during that conversation, she'd realized that she'd just have to live with that lump, to swallow it and hope it would disappear on its own at some point.

No calls, no emails, no Facebook messages, no letters, no Morse code with a flashlight during the dark hours of the night, no messages traced in window frost on a chilly autumn night, no burning thoughts so intense that they could penetrate fog and walls and doors. Nothing. Complete silence. It was as if the whole person had disappeared from the face of the earth. Or at least disappeared from Lumikki's life in one swift stroke. Just as unexpectedly and presumptuously as they'd come.

Lumikki remembered that day in May. The startlingly bright sunshine and the temperature stealing like a thief past seventy degrees for the first time all year. She was walking downtown with too many layers on. On the shore by the rapids, she took off her jacket and sat down on a bench to watch the dark water flowing by and feel the warmth of the sun on her face. It occurred to her that the moment would be perfect if she was eating her first ice cream cone of the season. Fortunately, an ice cream stand was right there next to her. Lumikki swung her jacket over her shoulder and went to stand at the end of the long line. Plenty of other people were craving their first cold treat too.

As she waited in line, Lumikki wondered whether she should get licorice or lemon. Licorice was her default choice. And it was good. But the lemon was also appealing. Maybe it was the May light and the sun promising a long summer of stifling heat. When her turn came, she still hadn't made up her mind yet.

Light blue eyes measured Lumikki as she opened her mouth to order. The ice cream seller was faster, though.

"Don't say anything. Let me guess. You don't want chocolate or strawberry. And definitely not vanilla. You aren't interested in that caramel fudge stuff or any of the new flavors that you mostly think are just a way to scam the stupid and the curious. You're a licorice girl. It's obvious from a mile away."

The light blue eyes narrowed a touch and then refocused.

"But right now, what you want is lemon. Because it isn't really spring anymore, but it also isn't quite summer yet. You want something sour and yellow. May sun ice cream."

Lumikki was speechless.

"You'll have one scoop, but you don't want a waffle cone because you think they taste like sweetened cardboard. So I'll put it in a little cup."

The ice cream seller turned to fill the order. Suddenly, Lumikki was unbearably hot. She would have been hot even if she'd stripped down to her underwear right then and there. He took so long. The awkward moment stretched out. Lumikki still hadn't been able to say anything. Finally, the boy turned and handed Lumikki a paper napkin and a bowl of ice cream. When Lumikki started digging in her pocket for money, a smile flashed in the light blue eyes.

"Don't worry about it. My treat."

Lumikki managed to splutter something resembling a thank-you and then spun on her heels with burning cheeks. She felt like she'd just been X-rayed. The feeling was extremely uncomfortable and also strangely tingly. When she returned to her bench by the rapids, she noticed something written on the napkin.

"Call. You know you want to." And a phone number.

Lumikki shook her head. *Presumptuous,* she thought. *And probably a jerk.* That night, she dialed the number with sweaty palms.

Selfish jerk. Pathetic coward. Good-for-nothing quitter. No matter how many times Lumikki repeated those words through the slow, endless hours lying awake at night after their breakup, they never turned true. She had loved a jerk, a coward, a quitter. She had understood his decision even though she didn't want to understand. She had waited and hoped, hoped and waited, jumping every time the telephone rang, sitting at her window looking down on the street, imagining she saw that familiar gait. She made strong black coffee in the middle of the night since she knew she wouldn't be able to sleep anyway. The pungent smell of the coffee was comforting, wrapping around her like a warm blanket. She drank the coffee too hot on purpose, trying to dissolve the lump in her throat.

Over weeks and months, the lump shrank and the longing eased into the background. She willfully gave up on hope. It wasn't any use. They'd probably never see each other again.

Lumikki began throwing water on the rocks in the sauna, dumping more and more until the stove stopped answering with an angry hiss. Hot steam painfully struck her upper back and neck. Lumikki straightened her back and felt the clenching in her stomach relent. Her eyes stinging, she wiped them with her hand. It was sweat, just sweat.

★　★　★

That evening, Lumikki stared at the white wall of her apartment and thought about the painting she was working on in art class. She wasn't a particularly gifted painter or illustrator, although she did love visual arts. She didn't hold out any hope of ever becoming more than a capable amateur. She took art classes just for fun, enjoying the chance to play and relax by making pictures. She doubted that later in life she'd have access to free paints, canvases, and a studio like the school offered.

Black, black, black. The surface had already been covered, but Lumikki had wanted even more black, more texture, cracks, and crevices so the painting wouldn't just be two-dimensional. Once she had enough layers, she laid the canvas out on the studio floor on top of some newspaper and, climbing onto a chair, began dripping red paint onto it. The drops of paint splashed against the black like red drops of rain, like drops of blood.

Lumikki had almost finished it today.

And now she knew the painting's title too. *Girlfriends.*

THURSDAY, MARCH 3

15

White, tufted, puffy, gauzy, like mountains of whipped cream. Far off and farther still, rolling over and under and past each other. Slowly, languidly moving clouds.

"Day cools towards evening time . . ." The words of a Swedish poem ran through her mind.

This day hadn't cooled off yet, but the worst of the heat had passed. The air was like nectar. As if stroking the contours of her body with a great feather, it caressed her toes, thighs, and arms. Out on the dock, they could lie completely naked, looking at the sky and the clouds. Waiting. Yearning. Longing for the other while still within arm's reach. Smiling, feeling that look on her skin.

"Take my slender, longing shoulders in your hands . . ."

Warmth from the air and from within. Warmth that dispelled idle thoughts. Hastening leisure, languid haste. The endless, endless transience of summer. The moment when everything was still good and being together was better than being alone. The thought that this feeling could last and last. *We could just stay here. I could be with this person. I could take that hand dozens, hundreds, thousands of times. And be quiet. Be quiet and hear our breath seek the same unforced, tranquil rhythm that could also get fast and urgent together, in sync.*

When summer had passed and a cold undertone appeared in the wind as it scattered the first yellow leaves from the birch trees, those thoughts felt like a dream. Like a dream someone else had dreamed.

Lumikki sighed and moved her gaze from the sky toward the police station. The large windows of the bus depot offered her an unobstructed view. This was her third hour of waiting for something to happen.

And it felt pointless.

In the bone-chilling cold, she had followed Elisa's dad, Terho Väisänen, from their home in Pyynikki to the highway. Then Väisänen had turned and gone to work, and Lumikki had taken up her watch in the bus depot. She wasn't about to wait at the police station itself. The passport-processing lines were famously slow, but a girl sitting in the waiting room for hours on end would have had to arouse suspicion at some point.

No one was glowering at her here, though. She was well groomed enough that she didn't look homeless, and she was inconspicuous enough that no one would even remember her being here.

Still, spending her day like this felt ludicrous. The most

likely scenario was that Väisänen would stay at work until four or later and then walk home along the same route he had come. Quite the daredevil stakeout.

Lumikki was on her fourth paper cup of black coffee. She had to stay awake somehow.

Money. Men chasing Elisa. The young woman in the photographs. Polar Bear.

How did everything connect?

Väisänen was the key. She was sure of that much. Elisa was sure too, even though she didn't want to believe anything bad about her dad. But she had to. After seeing the pictures, her face went somehow gray. Something inside her collapsed. In that moment, what remained of the innocence of her youth disappeared, and a part of her identity shattered.

Lumikki recognized the feeling. She remembered looking at herself in the mirror sometime in the fall of first grade, a little before Christmas, and seeing a frightened, shocked little girl who never could have believed that something like that could happen to her. That anything like that even existed. *I am no longer me.* That was what she had thought. And it was true. She had become something else, a different kind of girl.

Once upon a time, there was a girl who learned to fear.

Weary from watching the police station, Lumikki rested her eyes by looking around the bus depot for a while. Renovated about a year earlier, it was a beautiful Functionalist building. The morning light rippled in through large windows. If you only looked at the light and not at the dazzling brightness outside, you could imagine it was summer.

Lumikki would have liked to lean back in her waiting hall chair, close her eyes, and dream once more of warmth and abandon. To accept the joy and sorrow of those summer memories. What the hell was she doing here?

Viivo Tamm kept one eye on the police station as he filled in his tabloid sudoku. He was doubting Boris Sokolov's mental health. Lying in ambush all day for an on-duty police officer didn't feel all that smart. But Sokolov was sure that something funny was going on. He was puzzled by Väisänen's lack of response to Natalia's email. Apparently, Natalia had giggled once about how Väisänen usually replied to her almost before she had clicked send.

Sokolov had this hunch something was going to happen today. And when Sokolov had a hunch, there was no point arguing.

Viivo had asked Sokolov why he couldn't just go talk to Väisänen. To make him understand it wasn't a good idea to keep jerking them around. Viivo was good at keeping people in line. Keeping them quiet. Some people never said anything again after he paid them a visit.

Unfortunately, that wasn't an option this time. None of them could be seen with the cop if they wanted to continue their collaboration. So he was just supposed to watch.

Sokolov was convinced that Väisänen was trying to pull a fast one, and he wanted to know whether he had accomplices.

Did that square need a nine or a seven? Should have picked a three-star sudoku instead of a five. Keep it simple. He wasn't trying to become a sudoku master or anything, just kill some time. Chewing on the end of his pencil, Viivo glanced up at the police station.

This was going to waste his entire day.

Lumikki started digging out her cell phone to call Elisa and take back her promise. She had already wasted enough of her life on this futile stakeout.

Over in the police station, Terho Väisänen thought about the email he'd received late the night before. Of course, he hadn't been able to contact Polar Bear directly, but he did manage to get in touch with one of his "assistants," who also went by a code name. The assistant had emailed to say that Terho should visit the Tampere Convention Center to retrieve a cell phone hidden in the tank of the third toilet stall in the men's restroom, and use it to call the first number in the contact list. Then he would receive further instructions. The cell phone would be there today only.

Was he biting off more than he could chew?

Maybe he should just keep working with Boris Sokolov and the Estonians. They were straightforward midlevel criminals. Sokolov was a rung above the Estonians, but still just an underling. Polar Bear was something else entirely. There were only rumors about him, nothing concrete. Terho didn't know anyone who had actually seen the man.

But if he wanted his money, he had to do something. And he really wanted it. He had to have it. He had been counting on it, and now a couple of gambling debts were threatening to come due.

Pulling on his coat, Terho silenced his grumbling stomach and decided to spend his lunch hour in the convention center restroom.

A man walked out of the police station.

Viivo Tamm perked up.

Lumikki perked up.

Tamm was slightly faster, which was lucky for Lumikki because it gave her just enough time to realize that the man who suddenly dropped his sudoku looked familiar. When he sprang into action, Lumikki recognized him from the length of his stride, his slightly hunched posture, and the way he swung his arms.

One of her pursuers.

The man rushed out the door. In the blink of an eye, Lumikki understood that it was no accident that he was here and was charging out at the same time she was. A simple fact connected her and this man.

The same target.

Damn it. This was going to make everything more difficult. She would have to stay out of sight of two men instead of just one.

16

LUMIKKI STOOD IN THE LOBBY OF THE CONVENTION CENTER, momentarily indecisive.

So far, everything had gone well. Elisa's dad had been so focused on reaching his destination and his pursuer was so focused on tailing him that neither had paid any attention to Lumikki. She had hung back as far as she could, maintaining a visual connection with both men. Now you see me, now you don't. She knew this game from dodging bullies at school.

After crossing the railroad bridge, they each passed the university and turned north toward the convention center. Inside, Lumikki ran into a problem.

Terho Väisänen walked resolutely along the main concourse, following Kimmo Kaivanto's *Blue Line,* a stripe of special tiles running down the middle of the floor that occasionally rose toward the ceiling in blocky cobalt statues. Then Väisänen went into the men's restroom. His pursuer paused for a few seconds outside, glancing around and then entering as well.

Lumikki considered her options. She could wait in the lobby, hidden from view. However, something decisive might happen in the restroom. Would *probably* happen in the restroom. No way had Elisa's dad come all this way just to get a little variety in the color of tile he stared at while he peed. He had some other reason for being here, and Lumikki had to find out what that was. She couldn't go inside as a girl because she would attract too much unwanted attention. So she would have to go in as a boy.

Lumikki looked at herself in the mirrors next to the coat check. She was wearing dark clothing and a gray knit hat. All appropriately gender neutral. A thick winter coat concealed the shape of her body. Quickly tucking her hair under her hat, she changed her posture, shifting her center of gravity slightly. She altered the expression on her face.

The transformation was striking. In the mirror, a teenage boy with his hat pulled down low glared back at her.

The gait was the most important thing. She had to relax, opening her hips and slouching slightly. Then she walked up to the men's room door, grabbed the handle, and yanked it open confidently.

Terho Väisänen's fingers slipped when he tried to lift the lid of the toilet tank. It was surprisingly heavy and tight-fitting. He tried to get his fingernails into the tiny gap, but it didn't help. He needed something longer. Terho rummaged in his pockets. His reflector armband wasn't going to be any help, and neither was his driver's license. Fortunately, in the bottom of one coat pocket, he found the key to an old bike lock, which he was able to wedge under the lid. Then he started wrenching the tank open as quietly as possible. Suddenly, he heard someone enter the stall on his left.

Just his luck. Couldn't he ever catch a break?

The key was bending dangerously, but thank goodness, the lid was also shifting. It banged nastily against the edge of the tank, sounding like an explosion in the quiet restroom.

The door opened again. Great, another set of ears. The newcomer chose the stall on his right. Terho felt surrounded. He had to calm down, breathe deeply, try not to be paranoid. The convention center was a public place with free toilets. Of course there would be other people here. It was just an unfortunate coincidence that three men wanted to empty their bowels at the same time. Well, two, since he was otherwise occupied.

Terho removed his coat and rolled up his shirtsleeves. Shoving his hand into the water tank, he groped around. At first, his fingers only felt water, and he was revolted, despite knowing that tank liquid was perfectly clean. Was he in the right stall? What if they had already taken the phone back? Or what if he had been tricked?

Then his hand hit something.

Bingo.

Terho pulled out a black case, which must have been waterproof. Opening it carefully, he found a cell phone wrapped in plastic inside. Shoving the phone in one coat pocket and the case in another, he replaced the toilet tank lid. His heart was pounding in his ears like an insane drummer. He realized his hands were shaking. Fear made his knees weak, even though there shouldn't have been anything to be afraid of.

Coat on, door open, quickly to the sinks. Vigorously rubbing soap into his hands, Terho washed and rinsed thoroughly, and then repeated the process. He fought back his desire to wipe his fingerprints off the water tank. That would have been excessive.

Not a peep came from the other toilet stalls. *Maybe a little constipation going around,* Terho thought, drying his hands carefully and then hurrying out of the room.

Lumikki counted the seconds. With a quick glance down, she had made sure to enter a stall next to Väisänen. He'd been struggling with something, and based on the noises, it must have been the toilet tank. After finishing the job, he'd washed his hands and left.

She heard the pursuer flush. For the sake of appearances, presumably. Then he left the restroom too, but without washing his hands. Lumikki detested it when people didn't wash their hands after using the bathroom. She wasn't a clean freak by any means, but that was just basic hygiene.

Five, six, seven, eight . . .

At ten seconds, Lumikki opened the stall door, washed her hands, and rushed out. She made it just in time to see Terho Väisänen walk out of the building with the other man trailing behind. Lumikki had to hurry.

★　★　★

The park and duck pond outside looked enchanted. Every trunk and branch was either covered in thick rime or snow frozen in delicate crystalline formations. Sunlight reflected off every facet. Glittering, glimmering, glistening, sparkling, scintillating. The Snow Queen had ridden her sleigh through the park with hair and gown streaming, leaving behind infinitesimal ice crystals suspended in the air. She had made everything white and magical.

The breath of the Snow Queen. Ice and wind.

Lumikki's breath. Water vapor that quickly formed frost on her scarf and the delicate, almost imperceptible hair of her cheeks.

Stopping at some exercise equipment along the jogging path, she did a few pull-ups, eavesdropping carefully. Terho Väisänen had removed a cell phone from his pocket, fiddling with it for a few seconds before walking toward the pond with it pressed to his ear.

His pursuer stood behind a nearby tree pretending to light a cigarette. It seemed like Väisänen still hadn't noticed him. He'd probably notice Lumikki doing her pull-ups, but he wouldn't think some kid out for a jog would be interested in his telephone conversation. He also probably thought he was far enough away that no one could hear. However, in the perfectly still winter air, sound waves carried a long way.

Three, four, five.

Lumikki counted pull-ups while she waited for Elisa's dad to start his call.

"Hello? This is . . . okay, you know who this is."

The English made understanding harder. Väisänen spoke

in a low voice facing the pond, which meant some of the words got lost along the way. Filling in the gaps would have been easier in Finnish.

Lumikki's arms began to tire. She obviously hadn't been doing enough pull-ups lately. She didn't give up, though.

The pursuer was clearly listening too.

Twelve, thirteen.

"Polar Bear . . . So soon? Eight p.m. tomorrow. Right. Black tie. If you could just—"

The last sentence was cut off. Someone had clearly hung up on Terho Väisänen. Lumikki had heard enough, though. Elisa's dad was going to Polar Bear's party after all.

Lumikki's arms suddenly failed her, sending her thudding to the ground, muscles trembling and sore from the exertion.

Crap. So much for staying invisible.

Väisänen and his pursuer both turned to look in her direction. There was no way she could continue following them. Now the most important thing was to suck it up and finish playing her role as the innocent athlete.

Lumikki started jogging around the duck pond, trying to maintain her masculine posture. Her combat boots slipped on the icy walking path, breaking the illusion. But they weren't going to turn into cleated running shoes simply because she willed them to. She just had to keep her chin up.

Nothing to see here, folks. Just a kid out for a run.

If she could only get around the pond, she would have a straight shot home to a cup of something warm and a chance to report back to Elisa.

Lumikki knew her hope was in vain when she heard heavy footfalls approaching from behind.

17

Boris Sokolov tried to call Viivo Tamm, but he didn't pick up. He'd probably put his phone on silent to focus on the stakeout. That was sensible, but the whole job was pointless now. Boris had just received a message from Polar Bear saying that Terho Väisänen had gotten in contact with him, and that Polar Bear's men had delivered an invitation to the party by rather unorthodox means. Boris didn't always understand Polar Bear's methods. Sometimes he wondered whether Polar Bear was really so cautious or just liked running people around. The latter possibility felt as plausible as the first. Following Polar Bear's orders could be exhausting. Boris knew he was in a privileged position, even a favorite of sorts, but that could be taken away at any moment. He lived in constant fear, an invisible noose around his neck. He didn't have room for a single mistake.

So he needed to stay focused on the job at hand. And now

there was no reason to risk someone connecting the Estonian to their police informant. Or Tamm doing something stupid. Viivo was a good man, a professional, but occasionally he lost his cool. When that happened, he could become unpredictable and difficult to control.

Boris sent him a text message. It said: *"Stop. Abort mission."*

Viivo Tamm sped up. This time the little bitch wasn't going to get away from him. This time he would show her. The first time had been a fluke. Now it was personal. His cell phone buzzed in his pocket. Someone was trying to call, but Viivo couldn't stop to answer just now. He had business to attend to.

At first, Viivo hadn't been able to put his finger on what was so familiar about the boy at the pull-up bar. Then he looked closer. The coat. He had seen it somewhere before. When the boy started running, Tamm remembered. The boy wasn't a boy; he was a girl. A girl running a little differently somehow, but similarly enough that he recognized her.

But why hadn't Terho Väisänen recognized her? His own daughter?

Processing this took Tamm a few seconds, but when the insight came, it hit him like a ton of bricks. The girl wasn't the cop's daughter. This girl was someone else entirely who was somehow mixed up in all of this. And Viivo was going to find out how.

When the girl sped up, Viivo filled with rage. No teenage bitch was going to cross him. Because of her, he had frozen his fingers and toes, using up precious time he could have spent dealing product, skulking around in the bushes in Pyynikki, and filling in sudoku puzzles in the bus depot. The girl in the red hat had made a fool of him.

He was going to catch her and lean on her until she told him what her connection was.

She was going to learn not to play grown-up games when she didn't know the rules.

Up along a narrow path flanking the convention center, up-hill toward Kaleva Street and over it. Ice, slippery, completely the wrong shoes for running. Lung-rending cold and a bulky coat. Winter running clearly wasn't her sport.

Lumikki glanced back.

The man had nearly caught up with her.

Lumikki tried to breathe through a gap in her teeth. Hissing as she ran, like she was messing up a tongue twister. *She sells seashells by the seashore.* The frigid air was merciless.

Across Kaleva Street to the other side.

Cold, cold, cold, cold. Cold hands, cold heart. Cold hands, cold heart. Words pounded in Lumikki's head as she tried to think rationally. Should she continue along Kaleva Street? Pluses: other people, cars. Minuses: patches of black ice and the possibility that the pursuer's accomplices could be lurking somewhere with their van, ready to nab her at any second. Would they dare? In broad daylight?

Lumikki made a quick decision as she reached the next cross street. The walking path was less icy there. Turning, she ran toward the graveyard.

The man followed. Fortunately, he seemed to be having trouble with the slippery spots too.

Cold hands, cold heart . . .

Stop it.

Lumikki tried to get something else stuck in her head.

Sheryl Crow came to the rescue.

Lumikki's combat boots kept slipping. She swore to herself. From now on, she would have to start wearing ice cleats and running shoes all the time. Just in case someone started chasing her. Which seemed more than a little likely in light of recent events.

She turned into the cemetery, speeding past Väinö Linna's grave on the right, Juice Leskinen's on the left. Dead writers and singers might be able to save her from boredom on long winter nights, but they couldn't do anything for her now. Was she really going to die surrounded by graves? How ironic.

She could hear the steps growing closer all the time. Lumikki knew looking over her shoulder was not a good idea now. If she did, she would lose precious seconds. Could she run to the chapel? Or to the crematorium pickup door? Would someone be there? Could she get inside?

No running in cemeteries.

Her mother's voice. Her mother's rules. *Sorry, Mom. Not even you can know or control everything. Sometimes you just have to run.*

The dead don't care. The dead are dead. Corpses don't care even if the girl running over their graves is trying not to become a corpse herself. That was why she had to run, even though her feet slipped wildly with each step, even though the cold seemed to be filling her lungs with tiny puncture holes and her back was wet under her heavy coat and sweater.

The tall spruces of the graveyard were frosted with white, softening their sharp lines. Their branches hung down under the weight of the snow, down toward the headstones, down toward any visitors.

The dead and the living. The living and the dead.

Come again to judge.

The living and the dead.

Lumikki could already hear the man's breathing. Not long until his hand would grab the back of her coat.

Then something happened. Lumikki heard a thud, a snarled cry, and a string of curses in Estonian. She didn't understand them, but the meaning was clear. She didn't turn, but hope gave her legs renewed strength.

Slipping and falling, Viivo Tamm banged his left knee painfully on the ice. Immediately, he knew the game was up. He wasn't going to be chasing the girl anymore. He would be lucky to be able to limp back home.

Like a whipped dog.

Like a beaten-down mongrel.

Again his rage boiled up inside. But now it was bigger, redder, and more blinding. Propped on one knee, he drew his pistol.

He didn't think; he only felt with every fiber of his being that the girl had to be stopped. At any cost. He raised his weapon and aimed.

★ ★ ★

Lumikki heard a muffled crack. Then something whizzed past her thigh and struck a gravestone ahead of her, blasting a piece off.

A bullet.

The man was shooting at her.

Lumikki's pulse suddenly jumped twenty beats higher. Now she flew, no longer noticing the slippery ground or the cold air or the rivulets of sweat running down her spine.

Only after a long, long way did she dare to take a look back. The man's silhouette was small but still visible, holding his knee. Some friendly old lady had gone to help him.

There was no sign of the gun. No more bullets whizzed at her.

Lumikki continued running, which suddenly felt easy. She knew she had escaped.

This time.

Cracks ran through the paint on the ceiling, forming strange roads to nowhere. Lumikki lay on her bed, looking at the crisscrossing lines and letting the anger inside her grow. Against her stomach, she clutched a worn-out baby-blue stuffed rabbit that was missing an ear. The bunny accepted the hard, desperate grip of her hands.

She had made it home, yanking off her combat boots and hurling her winter coat at the back of a chair. After stripping off her soaked sweater and the even wetter long-sleeved shirt underneath, she stood in the shower for half an hour, letting the water wash over her like heavy rain. She washed her hair with unscented shampoo and used similarly fragrance-free soap. She always used odorless products. Not because she was allergic or had especially sensitive skin, but because she didn't want to smell like anything in particular.

Recognizing a person from the shampoo, soap, or lotion they used was all too easy, not to mention perfume or aftershave. Just a hint of a fruity soap could be enough to tell even a stuffed-up nose that a certain person had just been in the room. Most people couldn't identify other people's characteristic odors in public spaces—that took a more developed sense of smell—but anyone who didn't have the flu could pick out the cloying, pungent smells of perfumes.

Scents also triggered memories. The smell of pine tar shampoo brought back a summer night and dragonflies flitting over the surface of the water. Musky shower gel traced a sharp picture of wiry, muscular arms and a back with beautiful, prominent shoulder blades. It reminded her of the moments they lay embracing, laughing at some little thing no one else would think was funny at all. It made her think of the sharp, searching gaze of those light blue eyes, before which she always felt bewildered and flushed. Her heart skipped a beat and her knees went momentarily weak whenever someone walked past smelling of that shower gel. Even though she saw—and knew even before seeing—that the smell was not coming from the person she longed for. That's how strongly smells affect memory.

A person might not remember how a stranger looked, but when you happened to smell his aftershave somewhere else, his burly frame, short hair, jeans, and checked button-down shirt immediately appeared in your mind. For example, she might remember how this man walked and where. Whether he entered a certain door.

Lumikki didn't want that. She didn't want strangers remembering her. Or even, necessarily, all of her acquaintances. She wanted to be able to move around as invisible and scentless as possible.

Lumikki had rinsed the fear and panic from her skin. She had treated the blisters brought on by running in boots.

She had answered a call from her mom.

"Fine. No, school isn't too bad. Yes, I still have money."

Lies. Well-intentioned lies.

When did she stop telling her mother everything? When she started school? That was probably it. Or maybe even earlier, since her family didn't talk much in general. Lumikki had never figured out everything they didn't talk about, but the lack of talking hung so thick in every room that it attacked you like cobwebs. Everyone minded their own business. The taboo topics could be completely bizarre, things an outsider would never guess in a million years. Like the stuffed animal Lumikki was holding. Mom had brought it to her the last time she visited Tampere and said that it was Lumikki's favorite toy as a child. Looking at the bunny's jet-black eyes, Lumikki instantly remembered that it had really been someone else's favorite. Not hers, though she had played with it too. She had expressed the thought out loud.

"No, you must be remembering wrong," Mom had said. "This was your favorite toy, and his name was Oscar."

Lumikki had shaken her head.

"I gave him the name Oscar later. At first, his name was Zany. Maybe I got him from a cousin or something."

Mom didn't say anything, and Lumikki had taken that to mean that this was one more of the many things they simply weren't going to talk about.

The cracks in the ceiling were like a star chart for a foreign sky. Flaws. She loved them. They were interesting. But right now Lumikki was concentrating on anger, because it gave her power. She had been chased a second time, and now someone had shot at her. By all rights, she should want even less to do with this mess than before. But now she wanted to know; she wanted clarity; she wanted closure. And most of all, she wanted these men to pay for their crimes. She didn't want to be afraid anymore.

The fear would only end once the last card was revealed, though, and no one else was going to turn it over for her.

That was why she knew what she intended to do the following day. Angrily hurling the bunny rabbit in the corner, she pulled out her phone and called Elisa.

With the aid of a cane, Viivo Tamm hobbled to his door and struggled with the key. Holding the cane and turning the key while avoiding putting any weight on his left leg was difficult. Swaying off balance, he grimaced.

The excessively helpful old lady at the cemetery had practically forced him to call an ambulance and probably would have come along to make sure everything was all right if the paramedics hadn't assured her that Viivo was in the best possible hands.

After finding a hairline fracture on his X-ray, the ER doctor fitted him with a splint and sent him off with a cane and some strong painkillers.

Now he was finally home. Viivo couldn't remember his barren, dreary little studio apartment ever feeling so inviting. A cold beer, a couple of ibuprofens, and maybe some of the doc's super pills. Mixed drug use at its best. Then he'd call Sokolov, who had already left several angry messages on his voice mail.

Raving lunatic Russian. He felt like ignoring the calls, but then Sokolov would come banging on his door.

A musty fug greeted Viivo in the entryway. At some point, he really should wash the mountain of dishes in the sink. But there was also a strange hint of peppermint mixed in. As if someone had just eaten a piece of hard candy in the apartment.

Closing the door, he limped into his combination living room—bedroom—office. He didn't have time to turn on the light, though, because someone did it for him.

Viivo did have time to register the meaning of the smell.

Polar Bear's men.

The shot was only a muffled snap. Then Viivo fell on his back, and blood welled up out of his mouth like red paint.

FRIDAY, MARCH 4

18

Skin as white as snow.

An enormous powder brush swept over Lumikki's face. She was pale after the long winter, but they weren't trying to hide it. Quite the opposite. The foundation cream was a step lighter than her natural skin tone. As was the powder. The color shift was hidden carefully under the arc of her jaw. The makeup equalized the color of her skin and concealed the small blemishes, making her face unnaturally smooth. She looked like a porcelain doll.

Lips as red as blood.

Elisa carefully traced the outline of Lumikki's lips. The liner pencil ran along her cupid's bow, then the left side of her upper lip, and finally the right. Then came the lower lip with one sure stroke. Fading the lines toward the middle of the lips. That enhanced the impression of depth.

One layer of lipstick. Excess carefully removed with a

paper towel. Then another layer. And finally, red lip gloss in the middle to create an optical illusion of plumpness.

Hair as black as ebony.

Elisa arranged Lumikki's bangs and then froze them with a fine mist of hairspray. Fluffing the rest of her bob cut, Elisa let another layer of hairspray fix it in place.

The hair dye had taken well. Lumikki thought about how strange it had looked when she washed her hair after giving the dye time to set and blue-black rivulets had snaked across the white tile. The dye had formed beautiful, otherworldly patterns on the floor until the drain sucked the tinted water down the pipes. Lumikki had rinsed her hair until the water ran perfectly clear.

Even stranger had been when Elisa sat her down in a chair, wrapped an old sheet around her shoulders, and started trimming her hair. First to her shoulders and then up a little below her ears. Black locks pattered to the floor. It took Lumikki a while to get used to the idea that they were coming from her head.

Wet black strands of hair curling on the floor. Like question marks without the dot. The whole situation was a question mark. Lumikki longed for that missing period, something to put a full stop to everything that had been happening. That was why she was here.

"You aren't regretting this, are you?" Elisa had asked in the middle of the makeover. Lumikki almost smiled.

"Hair's just dead cells."

Elisa shivered. "I could never think like that."

Last, Elisa had given her bangs, straightened her hair, and

double-checked to make sure there weren't any stray strands poking out.

Elisa handed Lumikki a long red evening gown whose color shimmered from rose to orange and purple to burgundy as the fabric shifted and the light caught it in different ways. Lumikki put it on. The evening dress was simple, with thin straps and lines that draped perfectly on her form.

Lumikki lifted her eyes.

Mirror, mirror, on the wall . . .

The beautiful woman who looked back at her was a stranger with erect posture, mysterious dark eyes, and an expression on her lips that could presage a smile or contempt. Lumikki was satisfied. This woman was not her. This woman was someone else. Someone who could get into Polar Bear's party.

Elisa bounced up and down, making strange little squeaks. Lumikki interpreted them as positive feedback.

"Oh my God, you're beautiful! I am so good. What the heck am I doing in high school when I could be the world's best makeup artist?"

Seeing Elisa happy felt good. The color had returned to her cheeks, and there wasn't that muzzy, forlorn emptiness lurking right behind her eyes.

"And now a touch of this," Elisa said, and then spritzed Lumikki's neck with perfume that Lumikki instantly recognized as Elisa's signature Joy.

Lumikki held her breath to avoid inhaling any of the mixture of essential oils and alcohol wafting in the air.

Now she smelled like someone other than herself as well.

Good. No one would remember her from the party. What they would remember was a woman who looked like Snow White from the fairy tale and smelled like expensive perfume, hairspray, and luxury soap.

"Guys, come look!"

Tuukka and Kasper clattered in from the adjoining room.

"Well, were you able to get her—Wow!" Tuukka stopped midsentence when Lumikki turned around.

Kasper's mouth literally hung open. "Um . . . wasn't it a different story where the dirty, mousy girl turns into a hot chick?" Kasper finally said. "Cinderella?"

"I'd hit that," Tuukka said.

He clearly hadn't had time to think before the words tumbled out of his mouth.

"In your dreams," Lumikki volleyed back, restraining herself.

It was 7:20 p.m. Three hours earlier, Lumikki had come over to Elisa's house, where Tuukka and Kasper were already waiting. The beginning of their meeting had been taciturn. They all knew that they had crossed some sort of line. Until this point, everything had been light, somehow, controllable— exciting, but not too exciting. It was different now. Someone had shot at Lumikki, and she was going to a place where her life could truly be in danger.

Lumikki had told them her plan.

It wasn't sensible. It wasn't rational. It was dangerous. Lumikki didn't care. She wanted to be in danger now. She wanted to move toward what frightened her most.

When Lumikki got to the place in her plan where she would try to get into the party secretly through the back, Kasper opened his mouth and said, "You won't be able to."

"How do you know?" Elisa asked.

"You don't just 'sneak in through the back' to get at Polar Bear. From what I've heard, they're going to have serious security there. Fences and guards and cameras and all that shit."

Kasper clasped his hands behind his neck and leaned back in his chair. He was clearly enjoying his role as the fount of all knowledge.

"Okay. Then we can forget the whole plan," Lumikki said sarcastically.

Kasper smiled slyly.

"Except that you can walk right through the front door with everyone watching."

"And how is that going to work?"

"Because women can. At least, the kind of young women they invite to the parties to keep the men company and look pretty. Just so long as you're dressed for the theme, no one is going to ask them anything. And this time, the theme is fairy tales."

Tuukka snarfed sparkling water out of his nose.

"Are you serious? Do you really think we can make our little eco-anarchist lesbo look like some kind of high-class whor—sorry, I mean . . . escort?"

Elisa appraised Lumikki from head to toe. Then she announced that the boys could go entertain themselves for a couple of hours watching movies or playing video games.

"I'll bet there are some things I can do that you two boneheads can't," she said with a smile. "And if Dad comes home, keep him out of my room. Say I'm sleeping or doing naked yoga or something."

By the time Lumikki was ready, it was 7:45. She had on her red gown and white high heels. She had practiced in them for a few minutes until she learned how to balance her weight between her legs and how to walk, which was completely different than in low-heeled shoes. When all was said and done, it wasn't that hard. This was just another role for her to play, adjusting her own movements to match the image created by the clothes.

Lumikki doesn't know how to walk normally. She always shuffles around. She's so weird.

Words from ten years before. Lumikki remembered precisely the tone of voice in which they had been delivered. The expressions and gestures that emphasized the words. The exaggerated mimicry.

In that moment, she had decided to learn to walk every possible way. Normally and abnormally, beautifully and unattractively, quickly and slowly, sauntering and mincing. So that no one would ever get to say anything like that to her again. It hadn't saved her then, but the skill had served her many times since.

Elisa helped Lumikki put on a short imitation fur coat and then handed her long black gloves that reached to her elbows. Finally, a small beaded handbag.

"Don't lose that. It's crazy expensive," Elisa said.

From downstairs, they heard banging around as Elisa's dad prepared for the party as well. Tuukka and Kasper had gone downstairs, preparing to go out. Lumikki snapped the purse open. Inside was face powder, blood-red lipstick in a gold tube, one hundred euros, and something fluffy and pink. Grabbing the fluffy surface, Lumikki felt her fingers sink in and then meet something hard. She lifted the object out of the purse. Pink handcuffs.

Elisa shook her head, blushing.

"Don't ask. I don't want to remember that party."

Lumikki raised her eyebrows ever so slightly and then put the handcuffs back in the bag. What Elisa did at her parties and with whom was none of Lumikki's business.

"And then this."

Elisa handed Lumikki a long black hooded parka that reached almost to her ankles.

"I don't know what I was thinking when I bought this. I look like I'm wearing a sleeping bag when I put it on. But now we have a use for it."

Lumikki put the parka on. It was a little tight in the sleeves with the fur coat underneath, but otherwise perfect. Fastening the snaps, she carefully pulled the hood over her hair and looked at herself one last time in the mirror.

The Abominable Snowman's black cousin, I presume.

Elisa and Lumikki stood facing each other for a few seconds. Neither had any words. Lumikki wanted to hug Elisa and tell her everything was going to work out fine. Even though she wasn't at all sure of that. And she had never wanted to hug anyone voluntarily, except maybe her mom and dad when she was little.

Elisa was afraid. So was Lumikki.

Elisa was ready to do her part. So was Lumikki.

Asking Elisa whether she was sure she wanted to dig any deeper into her father's business was pointless now. The time for questioning and hesitation had passed. Elisa might be a spoiled teenager who'd thought she was living the dream of a high school debutante. Maybe she used to think she could skip through life buying designer clothes and purses with her daddy's money, throwing out-of-control parties that someone else would clean up after, and tossing back drinks with a couple of pills on the side, toying with boys and men alike at will. By burying her frailty behind a makeup mask. By pretending to be dumber than she was.

But Lumikki saw that Elisa knew this night was going to change everything. That it would shatter her rose-tinted fantasies once and for all. The first cracks had formed last Sunday night when Elisa removed her hands from that plastic bag and wondered why they were so sticky. But what would be revealed on this night could never be washed away by water and soap.

A moment of determination flashed in Elisa's eyes, making Lumikki wonder whether they were really so different after all. Their worlds were never going to match up entirely, but in fleeting moments like these, they shared the same sliver of reality, the same feelings and thoughts.

Elisa filled her lungs and then exhaled calmly.

"Now I'm going to go hug my daddy good-bye," she said.

Lumikki nodded. The clock said 7:52.

19

TERHO VÄISÄNEN'S FINGERS SLIPPED ON THE SMOOTH SATIN AS
he tried to adjust his bow tie. His hands wouldn't stop sweating, and he had to keep drying them with toilet paper.

It was already so late. He should have been outside, waiting for the car to pick him up. Under no circumstances did he want to be late. The car wouldn't wait. The opportunity would pass, slipping through his fingers like this satin tie.

A black-tie occasion. When was the last time he'd worn a tux? Years ago at a party his wife's boss threw. He would never forget the five hours of uninterrupted pretentiousness, from the welcoming toast to the moment their taxi picked them up at the end of the night. He didn't like this kind of upper-crust soirée. Although in many regards, he was part of the "upper crust" these days too.

Finally, the bow tie cooperated. Fidgeting, he combed his hair one more time, even though the barber had just arranged it perfectly. Terho realized he was more nervous than he had been in ages. He reminded himself he was only going to the party for two reasons.

To speak directly to Polar Bear and, hopefully, to see Natalia.

She still hadn't replied to any of his emails. Terho knew that she had been to Polar Bear's parties before, but she was never willing to tell him anything about them.

Top secret, my love.

Polar Bear's grip on people could be uncanny. Terho doubted he would have any kind of bargaining position in the big boss's eyes. After all, he was just a pathetic narcotics cop, a bit player. Over the past ten years, he may have done his own small part in helping Polar Bear's businesses, but they probably would have gotten along just fine without him. Still, he had to try.

In the early hours of the previous morning, he had made a decision. He didn't want to go on. He wanted out of his double agent role. But in order for that to work, he needed some sort of compensation from Polar Bear to help patch the gaping hole that would leave in his future income. He had to be able to pay off his gambling debts and arrange things for Natalia and himself. Then he could focus on living an ordinary, peaceful life without anything to raise his heart rate. No crime, no gambling, no Natalia, no money.

He'd realized that he couldn't handle the stress and fear anymore. The secrecy that as a younger man had kept him high on an adrenaline buzz now just made him tired. He might be able to go on for a few more years, but then his health would give out. Maybe it would be his heart or maybe it would be his nerves, but either way, he was headed for a crash. He had been deluding himself for far too long already.

Terho stared at the man in the mirror, who looked older than his years. The bags hanging under his eyes, the loose skin hanging under his jaw, the belly hanging over his belt. Everything about him hung slack or overflowed. Years of stress and guilt ate at him, making him consume whatever passed in front of his mouth, neglect his health and well-being, neglect even his family. He had to admit that. If not to anyone else, at least to himself.

It had to end. Seeing Natalia also had to end. Given their shared past, they would never be able to appear in public together. He had to start a new, honest life. Which was why he was about to try something so reckless and unlikely to succeed. He intended to blackmail Polar Bear.

Terho glanced at his watch. Time to leave. He was just striding into the entryway when Elisa came tumbling down the stairs, grabbed his arm, and started dragging him toward the basement.

"What now? I should have left already," Terho said irritably.

"I need to show you something really important. It'll only take a minute."

"Not now. I can't be late. I have a really, really important event to attend."

"How can some party be more important than me?"

Elisa kept a firm grip on her father's arm, and she looked at him with large, accusatory eyes. Now, instead of his seventeen-year-old daughter, what Terho saw was the little seven-year-old Elisa he could never stand to disappoint.

"Okay. One minute."

Lumikki slipped quietly down the stairs, which was surprisingly difficult in high heels and the constricting sleeping bag coat. Tuukka was waiting for her outside, hidden near the gate.

"Not here yet," he whispered.

"Hopefully they aren't late," Lumikki said. The temperature was just a few degrees below freezing, a high for this winter.

A thin white layer of frost covered every surface. Houses, trees, rocks, cars. Clothing, hair, cheeks, thoughts.

"Elisa promised to keep her dad busy until I call," Tuukka said.

Then they fell silent and waited. Lumikki wondered why Tuukka didn't make some lewd wisecrack about her black snowman costume or the propositions she was sure to get during the course of the evening. Then she noticed the tension in his jaw. Tuukka was nervous. Maybe even afraid. Probably for the first time in his life, really.

Once upon a time, there was a boy who learned to fear.

Lumikki felt surprisingly calm. She was just following a set program. All she had to do was concentrate on her next move.

At 7:58, a black Audi turned onto the street and stopped in front of the house. Tuukka looked at Lumikki, one eyebrow raised. She nodded. Tuukka started walking. He walked casually past the black car and then, once he was outside of the driver's field of vision, hid behind another vehicle parked farther down the street and began creeping back toward the Audi. When he got behind the car, he stopped and waited.

Enter Kasper.

Starting at the corner, the boy walked toward the black car and then turned to walk in front of it. The driver did not react in any way. Removing a key from his pocket, Kasper showed it to the driver with an exaggerated flourish, pressed it with relish against the hood, and continued walking. The screech of metal on metal cleaved through the otherwise quiet winter evening. At first, the driver stared at Kasper as if not comprehending what was happening.

Kasper lifted his middle finger gleefully.

Then the driver came to life. Bellowing something incomprehensible, he sprang from the car. With the driver distracted, Tuukka acted with lightning speed and opened the trunk of the car a crack. Kasper was already running away, laughing maddeningly as the driver charged after him, turning only momentarily to lock the car with his key remote and then continuing to chase Kasper, who was running just slowly enough to remain temptingly close.

Lumikki was immediately at the car. Tuukka helped her into the trunk. Luckily, it wasn't one of the smaller ones, but Lumikki still had to arrange her arms and feet carefully in order to fit. Finally, she put a strip of silk fabric over the locking mechanism and gave Tuukka a thumbs-up to signal that everything was ready.

Tuukka replied with the same gesture and then closed the trunk as silently as possible.

When the darkness engulfed Lumikki, she had to fight

against a moment of panic. She was in an uncomfortable, tight space that smelled like gasoline. She hoped the trip wouldn't take long.

Lumikki heard the driver return, cursing to himself. Chirp chirp, and the locks opened. The driver climbed in and slammed the door shut.

Lumikki squirmed to see whether she could get her cell phone out of the little handbag. Just barely. She looked at the clock on the phone, which said 8:05. The brief blue glow from the display momentarily dispelling the darkness did her good.

Then she heard steps approaching from the direction of Elisa's house. A car door opened.

"What took you so long?" the driver asked irritably in English.

"Sorry. Family business," Lumikki heard Terho Väisänen reply.

"Polar Bear hates it when people are late."

"Let's not waste any more time then."

Amen. Lumikki agreed completely with Elisa's father. She had no desire to spend any more time in this place and position than absolutely necessary.

The Audi growled to life.

"You have criminals on this street."

Lumikki could just barely make out the driver's words. They made her smile. But when the car accelerated and cold currents of air began whistling through the gaps in the trunk, she got serious.

There was no turning back.

20

THE DARKNESS WAS IMPENETRABLE. THERE WAS NO WAY through it. It gave no ground.

She would never get out. She would never get air. She would die.

Gravel pressed a pattern of tiny depressions into her back. She squeezed gravel in her hands, feeling the sharp edges of the tiny rocks, letting them dribble between her fingers.

"Let me go!" she screamed.

She had already screamed it ten times, a hundred times, a thousand times. She had hammered on the lid with her fists, kicked it with her feet, turned over and tried to lever it open with her back. Nothing.

They were sitting on it. Probably dangling their feet and taking turns sucking a lollipop, savoring its strawberry flavor. They were in no rush. They had all the power.

The tears had already dried in Lumikki's eyes. She was

starting to panic. She felt like if she didn't get out right that instant, she would suffocate.

She started to shriek. As loudly as she could. She thought of the calls of seagulls and the way they opened their beaks so wide. She was a gull. She screamed.

The louder the sound, the more alive. She became the sound. She was one with the sound. The same red, raging, shrill note.

At some point, she realized it wasn't dark anymore. The lid of the gravel box was open. She sat up and wiped her tears. Grit stuck to her cheeks, finely ground gravel.

There was no sign of them.

They were waiting for their next opportunity. They knew just as well as Lumikki did that one would come.

Lumikki slowly counted to ten.

She couldn't panic. She wasn't the same girl now as back then. She had changed. She had learned. She could stay in any small space for any length of time.

Everything had gone the way it was supposed to so far. Almost everything.

Yes, she had bruises from banging against the sides of the trunk on some sharp turns. Yes, her nose burned like it would be filled with the stench of gasoline for the rest of time. Yes, she was shivering with cold and numb from head to toe. But those were minor details.

The Audi had driven for thirty-five minutes, then slowed and finally stopped. Terho Väisänen exited the car first. Then the driver followed a moment later, locking the vehicle and leaving.

Lumikki had listened and then, when everything was quiet, she grabbed the silk strip with her stiff fingers and pulled evenly, pushing up on the trunk at the same time with her legs. The fabric she'd stuck in the lock mechanism was supposed to shift the latch out of place so she could get out.

The sound of ripping silk was the worst thing Lumikki had heard in a very long time.

Don't panic. Stay calm.

Lumikki felt with her fingers for where the fabric had ripped. She couldn't find it. Her fingers had lost almost all sensation, and the long gloves she was wearing made feeling even more difficult. Lumikki grabbed her left glove with her teeth and pulled it off. Then she shoved her fingers into her mouth to warm them until the blood started flowing again.

Another attempt.

Her fingers fumbled at the area around the lock and felt fabric. Lumikki knew that her wet fingertips would freeze again in seconds.

Yes. Oh yes. Just enough silk remained that she could still get a grip on it. Clinging to the fabric, she pushed up powerfully with her legs and pulled the cloth slowly, slowly, slowly and steadily toward herself.

The lock didn't open.

Lumikki clenched her teeth, pushing and pulling. She strained with all her might.

Click.

The lock gave way. The trunk opened. Holding it open

just a crack, Lumikki steadied her breathing. She listened. Just then, another car pulled in next to hers and stopped. The people inside got out.

"You might think about vacuuming your car sometime," a woman's voice said. "Look at my shoes. They were supposed to be pink."

"You're the one who wanted to be Sleeping Beauty. I think the evil stepmother would have worked just as well. You could have worn black shoes then," a man replied.

The couple's quarreling voices receded. Silence returned.

Lumikki lifted the trunk a little more and peered out. She was in some sort of small parking lot. Fortunately, the black Audi was right at the edge, in the shadows and a little behind some trees. No one was around just now.

With no time to spare, Lumikki peeled off her sleeping bag coat, pulled her glove back on, climbed out of the trunk, and quietly closed it again. She had to leave the parka. The driver would wonder about it the next day or whenever he next opened the trunk. Lumikki checked her hair with her hands. It felt like it was in miraculously good shape. Elisa hadn't exaggerated when she said the hairspray she used could work magic.

Powder compact out of handbag, mirror up. Quick check of makeup. Remove a little stray lipstick from one corner. Then she was ready.

Lumikki turned to look at the party venue.

Boris Sokolov inspected his creation and nodded. The Snow Queen looked just like she should. If seeing this didn't make

Terho Väisänen stop making trouble, Boris was willing to eat a gallon of ice cubes. In one sitting.

Boris felt an indefinable sorrow and simultaneous satisfaction. The reason for the satisfaction was clear. He was relieved. He had worked things out with Polar Bear, and he wasn't holding a grudge over Viivo Tamm's shooting.

It seemed that some of Polar Bear's men had spotted Viivo running amok with a gun in broad daylight in the cemetery. That just wasn't how things were done. It showed that the man had lost his touch, that he had started to slip. There was nothing to be done with a man who was slipping—on that Polar Bear and Boris agreed.

So Viivo had to be eliminated. It wasn't personal.

Boris looked at Natalia, whose brown eyes were open. Her face wore a confused, surprised expression.

Poor little Natalia, did you really think Big Bad Boris wouldn't find out about your escape plan? And then the money. That would have been stealing. And stealing, as we all know, is wrong. If you had just done what was right, everything would be different now.

Natalia, Natalia.

Snow Queen, frost on her lips.

The party could start.

Kasper's reports had been accurate. A tall stone wall surrounded the building, which itself was a large, three-story house from the early 1900s that appeared to be located out in the middle of the woods. Only a narrow road led through the forest to the house.

Lumikki wondered whether the house was even on any

maps. There were places that certain people wanted kept secret, and there were ways to make that happen.

Lumikki started making her way toward the gate, where guards appeared to be stopping people and asking them something. Lumikki tried to look as much as possible like the role she was playing. A high-class paid escort.

When Lumikki's turn came, she stepped past the guards, confidently yet slowly, in keeping with her station.

"*Hetkinen.* Stop," one of the refrigerator-sized men said, repeating himself in Finnish and English.

Lumikki's heart jumped. Was this where it would end?

"*Kännykkä.* Cell phone," the guard demanded, extending his hand.

Lumikki pursed her lips and then dug her phone out of her handbag, shoving it into the man's enormous, outstretched palm with a pout. You would have thought this was a much more important object than Elisa's old, cast-off phone. The guard slipped the phone into his bag, which, judging from the clatter, contained more than a few already. Then without asking her permission, he grabbed Lumikki's purse, inspecting its contents and then giving it back with a grunt.

A barely noticeable movement of his head signaled to Lumikki that she could go through. She ordered her legs not to shake from the cold and relief. She kept her head up. Walking along the icy path in high heels was pure masochism, despite the gravel that had been carefully spread around.

One step at a time. Calmly.

Around her, it was dark. Lumikki walked along a lane of light. The driveway was lined with luminarias whose flames flickered restlessly. At the end of the path was a door and, standing at the door, the epitome of an old-fashioned butler. Slicked-back hair and short white gloves. A language of gestures that simultaneously conveyed superiority and subservient civility. The man opened the door for Lumikki, bowing slightly. Lumikki stepped in.

She had succeeded.

She had really gotten into Polar Bear's party. Now she just had to find out what Elisa's dad was mixed up in.

21

ANOTHER WORLD. ANOTHER REALITY.

Colors, lights, sounds. Blue that in an instant changed to green and yellow. Orange that turned to undulating gold. Violet that grew into sinuous garlands of burgundy, lilac, and fuchsia. Music, the singing of mermaids, the sighing of forests, the tinkling of crystals, the forgotten echoes of deep caverns, the chamber orchestras of palaces and castles, the jingling of tiny bells, all sweeping over you, grabbing you from behind, disappearing, and then returning again.

Wonderland.

Soundscapes and lights and props skillfully transformed each of the large rooms into its own reality. From a dark forest abuzz with secrets, Lumikki stepped into a silver ballroom with walls encircled by genuine rose garlands. She walked through an undersea kingdom. She peered into a log cabin with a small chair, a medium chair, and a large chair.

The illusions entranced her so thoroughly that several seconds passed before she began to discern the details of the rooms properly. Servers bearing trays were everywhere. Of course, each room offered fantastical drinks appropriate to the theme. Some of the drinks seemed to smoke, and others shifted color from purple at the bottom to light blue at the surface. Some of the servers were dressed as fairy-tale characters, some as gold-painted living statues.

Guests wandered from room to room with drinks in their hands. Amidst the din of voices, Lumikki could pick out Finnish, English, Swedish, Russian, and maybe more. She might have heard Spanish too, but she wasn't sure. Most of the women looked just like her. Young and dolled-up and like they didn't know any of the other attendees. Kasper had been right. A lot of these girls were being paid. The actual guests were mostly middle-aged men, a few older and a few younger. There was also the occasional couple. Lumikki recognized the slightly wizened-looking Sleeping Beauty and her prince. Both of them could have used some beauty sleep. If not a full hundred years, at least a few hours.

Some of the guests' faces appeared vaguely familiar to Lumikki. Were they politicians? Businessmen? Hard to say.

Lumikki tried quickly to visualize how the spaces connected. The first two floors had been reserved for the party. The third floor had rooms for people to retire to "rest," and the basement was for the staff. Or at least that was where the servers took their empty trays and then returned with full ones.

"I don't imagine I could offer you one of these, could I?"

Lumikki turned to see a man holding two glasses. He

had been directing his words at her. He was graying slightly, but most people would have called him handsome. His eyebrows were dark, his eyes brown, and his suit extremely well tailored. Out of the corner of her eye, she registered from the tag intentionally left on the cuff that it was Hugo Boss. So he wanted to pay a lot for his suit, but he was old-fashioned when it came to brands. It fit the image. In terms of his age, he could practically have been Lumikki's grandfather.

The man bowed to Lumikki. Lumikki restrained her desire to step back from the stench of cigar and aftershave. That was Hugo Boss too. Apparently, the man wanted to triple underline the idea that he was a boss himself.

"Unfortunately, it has apple in it," the man said in a low voice, as if it were some great secret. "I assume that's poisonous to you Snow Whites."

A self-satisfied smile hovered on the man's suntanned face. He obviously thought he was extremely clever.

Lumikki searched her repertoire of facial expressions and chose a slightly stupid, flattered, flirtatious smile.

"Yeah. We're kind of allergic to it. But if you find me something else nice and strong and a little sweet, then we could talk some more."

"Something strong and warming for a cold night like tonight," the man said, laying his hand on Lumikki's bare arm in a caressing gesture.

The hand was clammy. Lumikki contained her shudder of disgust, restricting it to her thoughts.

"You read my mind."

"Your wish is my command," the man said. "Don't go anywhere."

"I'll try not to get lost in the woods. Or end up a house slave for seven undersized men."

The man's smile widened.

"And if someone tries to dress you in a corset that's too tight, I promise to take it off," he said, throwing her a wink.

Well now, the gray panther knew his Grimm. But familiarity with fairy tales wasn't going to score him any points with Lumikki. Or lead to any other kind of scoring. Lumikki watched as the man's back retreated. Then she slipped upstairs.

Terho Väisänen looked around. There was no sign of Natalia. His bow tie was uncomfortably tight around his neck. He loosened it.

Some of the guests made his eyebrows shoot up. *Is he really here? And him?* This material could have filled the pages of both national tabloids and a couple of gossip magazines to boot. He watched as a well-known politician nibbled the ear of an uncomfortable-looking Tinker Bell.

Terho knew that no one was going to breathe a word about the party to anyone. Polar Bear's men butchered snitches. And not just snitches, but snitches' families, relatives, lovers, and friends. Everyone knew it, and no one wanted to end up as a cautionary tale.

He saw a young woman dressed as Snow White. There was something vaguely familiar about her. Didn't Elisa have a dress a lot like that? Well, it must have been a popular style and not quite the one-of-a-kind the saleswoman had led them to believe when he bought it for her. More evidence that you never got quite what you wanted, even with heaps of money.

You could still get a lot with money, though. You could get your life straightened out. And that was why he was here.

While the first-floor rooms were beautiful, enchanting fairy-tale worlds, the rooms on the second floor were full of savage nightmares from the same stories. Trees whose limbs grabbed at passersby like hands. Swamp sirens that used their songs to lure men into bottomless pools. Sleep that even a prince's kiss couldn't break.

One room was black and contained a threatening illusion of flying crows cawing. Lumikki flinched and almost ducked to avoid the imaginary claws grabbing at her hair.

Inside the room were two servers dressed in black, carrying silver platters. On the platters were small shot glasses full of black liquid. The servers were talking in hushed tones. Lumikki wanted to hear what they were saying, so she stepped closer, trying to look like she intended to take one of the drinks.

"Where's Polar Bear?" one of the servers asked.

"Haven't you heard that he never comes until midnight?"

"He? I thought—"

The server shot the other a warning and extended his silver platter ever so slightly toward Lumikki. Lumikki took a shot glass, smiled, and turned her back.

"Polar Bear has a strict rule that everyone always has to say 'he,'" the server whispered.

Lumikki tipped the glass so the liquid just touched her lips and considered what she'd heard. She glanced at the large, ornate clock on the wall. Nine-fifteen. Almost three hours left.

The other aspect of the exchange was a mystery. Why

wouldn't they refer to Polar Bear as "he"? Strange. Presumably, that would be cleared up at midnight too.

If the party was any indication, Polar Bear seemed increasingly odd. He—or was he a he after all?—used vast sums of money to create unbelievable sets for a single night, but you could bet most of the guests were incapable of appreciating the lavish rooms. All that mattered to them was that the alcohol didn't run out and the girls were beautiful and open to flirtation. And maybe more.

Swine in black tie.

As if a thousand-euro suit and a twenty-thousand-euro watch gave you class. Or the right to act however you pleased. If you had money, there were no rules. If there were no rules, you were a king.

Suddenly, Lumikki felt sick to her stomach. She wanted to go home. She wanted to kick off these high heels and pull on the gray slippers her grandmother had knitted her. She even kind of wanted to fix herself a cup of tea, even though she usually thought it was pointless warm water. Right now, it would have felt calming and homey and reminded her of wallpaper with roses and her grandmother's gentle hands braiding her hair.

Lumikki carefully licked her lips. Licorice vodka, just as she'd suspected. The sharp, salty taste eased her nausea.

Remember, you aren't really here. This character is not you. Someone else is walking through these rooms in white high heels and a red evening gown. None of this can touch you.

Lumikki straightened her back. She wasn't here to have a good time. She had a job to do.

22

NATALIA WAS NOT COLD. SHE HAD BEEN DEAD FOR 128 HOURS. One hundred and twenty-eight hours was a laughably short time when a person was alive. Dead, it was even shorter. Natalia had lived for twenty years, three months, and two days. She would be dead for an eternity. Next to eternity, 128 hours was no time at all.

If Natalia had still been alive, would she have wanted to go back to the moment when Boris Sokolov first contacted her? Natalia had met him a couple of times with her boyfriend at the time, a dealer named Dmitri, and she knew that Sokolov was a big fish in the business. Not a high-level boss, but a boss nonetheless. He had influence. Sokolov invited Natalia to join his team. They needed a presentable-looking young woman with a brain unclouded by booze or drugs.

Would she have wanted to choose differently? If she hadn't said yes to Sokolov, she never would have come to

Finland, she never would have met Terho Väisänen, she never would have tried to run away with the money, and she never would have taken that bullet in her gut. She wouldn't be lying dead now at zero degrees, blank eyes staring into the darkness, blue lips slightly parted as if ready to whisper in your ear.

If Natalia had known what would happen, of course she would have declined. But back then, all she had known was that she didn't want to raise her daughter in an apartment that stank of mold and whose cardboard-thin walls let through the neighbors' earsplitting fights and equally boisterous make-up sessions. So she had agreed. That very same week, Sokolov arranged better living arrangements for Natalia, her mother, and little Olga.

A year passed. Natalia peddled drugs to the young, rich, and affluent of Moscow, feeling that she was one of them. Young, rich, and beautiful.

Life could have been good. Worth living. But in her nineteen years, Natalia had already learned that whenever everything was going right, something would always mess it up. That time, it had been an order to leave for Finland with Sokolov to run the business there. She had imagined she'd end up in Helsinki, where flying home would be relatively easy. Instead, they sent her to Tampere, which had seemed pitifully small the instant she arrived. Before, Sokolov had spent half of his time in Moscow and half in Tampere, but now he was moving to Finland full-time.

Orders from Polar Bear, Sokolov had said. That was the first mention Natalia had heard of Polar Bear. Later on, she was invited to Polar Bear's parties and realized how ridiculously small her role really was in the grand scheme of things. She was a trivial cog, replaceable at a moment's notice.

Natalia felt like a Martian in Tampere. She walked wrong and dressed wrong. Her rabbit-fur muff and high-heeled boots were over the top. People stared at her on the street. Men tried to offer her money, but not for drugs, for sex. At times, Natalia thought bitterly that the only way not to stand out from the locals was to wear a snowsuit in the winter and a tracksuit in the fall and spring, and to spend all summer sitting in Tammela Square eating black sausage with a baseball cap on your head and knock-off Crocs on your feet.

She didn't know anyone in the city other than Sokolov and his Estonian sidekicks. In the beginning, she called home every night, listening to little Olga's voice and then crying herself to sleep.

Sometimes she watched the Finnish high schoolers, who looked like absolute babies in her eyes, even though she was barely a year older herself. She wondered what it would feel like to live like them. To go to a coffee shop after school to debate whether something a cute boy had said meant he liked you or what a teacher might ask on your history exam. To deliberate over college options and consider taking a year off before going. To dream about moving out on your own, buying your own dishes, and making your bed with those fancy, Finlayson-brand sheets your grandparents gave you as a graduation present. To have an existential crisis over not knowing what you want to do when you grow up.

Then Natalia had met Terho, who was completely different from Sokolov and the Estonians, even though Sokolov said he was "one of us." A narcotics detective who had gotten tangled up in the business, a mole.

Terho and Terho's rough hands. The affection Natalia felt for him from their very first meeting. He was so shy, so sweet and insecure about how to speak to her and how he could touch her. Completely different from her previous boyfriends and all the other men who immediately forced her into whatever shape they wished, twisting and posing her like a mannequin.

Had it been love? It had at least felt like love. Natalia had felt safe with him. Terho talked about his home, his family, normal life. Natalia had known that she wanted a life like that too. Not this secrecy, this fear, the sensitive nasal membranes and needle marks in her groin. He had promised to fix things for Natalia, to help her out. For a long time, Natalia had believed him, but nothing ever happened. He'd been making empty promises, just like every other man in Natalia's life.

Promises that turned to lies the instant they left the mouth.

Natalia should have learned by now. Not to trust anyone but herself. To make her own decisions and accept the consequences.

That was why she decided to take the thirty thousand meant for Terho from Sokolov's house and disappear. She made a plan. She stole Sokolov's spare key without him noticing. She arranged a hideout in the countryside. Everything should have been easy. On Sunday, Sokolov and the Estonians were supposed to be gone all day, but they came home early. That was why Natalia Smirnova was lying dead now, in the dark, naked.

She was accepting the consequences of her decisions, consequences that were heavier than she could ever have imagined.

Natalia's life had been a series of seemingly unavoidable wrong decisions. Wrong decisions had been offered to her as right, presented on a golden platter smelling of roses. But she had never looked under the tray or past the person holding it to see the backdrop of white snow splattered with a shower of red droplets.

That was why Natalia Smirnova was lying alone now in the cold without feeling the chill.

Just as she had lain for the past 128 hours.

But even in death, she could not be at peace. Boris Sokolov still had one more job for her.

23

LUMIKKI HURRIED DOWN TO THE BASEMENT. SHE GLANCED BACK to see if the man had followed her. No, thank goodness. She'd managed to shake him.

She had just been sampling the dozens of different delicacies at the buffet when the man who had accosted her earlier surprised her from behind and demanded an explanation for her disappearance.

"The ways of womankind are inscrutable sometimes," she answered coquettishly.

The man suggested that they move upstairs to investigate her feminine wiles a little more closely. Lumikki begged him to let her eat first. In response, the man placed his hands on her hips and said that it would be a shame to ruin such a lovely, slender waist with excessive gluttony. Lumikki replied that she hadn't eaten all day and that he would probably prefer for her not to faint. The man laughed.

"You're probably quite the little wildcat once you get going."

Yeah, I'll scratch your eyes out, Lumikki thought, but settled for answering with a kittenish meow. Then she faked him out by handing him her plate to hold and saying she was going to powder her nose. He stood there looking satisfied, obviously imagining that he now had collateral in his possession that Lumikki couldn't get along without. *Jackass.*

In the basement, Lumikki looked around. Directly ahead was a large kitchen, where, judging from the sounds, cooks were working at full tilt to prepare more amazing dishes. She heard the sizzling of frying pans, knives chopping against cutting boards, and orders being shouted over the din. A steady stream of servers marched through swinging doors carrying trays, bowls, and large serving platters. Lumikki discreetly watched the flow of food from a dim corner of the room, tucked safely out of sight.

She had caught a few glimpses of Elisa's father, but he kept disappearing when she tried to follow him.

Now, as if on cue, she heard Terho Väisänen's voice from a nearby hallway. He was speaking English with someone. The other person's voice sounded familiar too, but Lumikki couldn't place it.

The voices came toward her. Then Lumikki realized. She had heard the other man's voice when she was being chased in the woods. The Russian.

Lumikki thought for a second. Should she just stay put and pretend she was lost or curious and that was why she was in the basement? Neither of the men would recognize her. It would attract attention, though. She was in the wrong place, and way too visible, which wasn't a good thing given what she was up to. She really didn't want any of these people recognizing her later on the street.

Lumikki tested the nearest door. It opened. She carefully peeked inside, but no one was in the room. All she could see were several large chest freezers and stacked plastic crates of alcohol. Some sort of extra storage room, probably. Slipping inside, she waited for Väisänen and the Russian to pass the door.

They didn't. Instead, they stopped.

"I've got something to show you," Lumikki heard the Russian say in English.

She glanced around. No back door. No place to hide. Nowhere she could go and no way to get out.

Nowhere but the freezers.

Lifting the lid of the closest ice chest, she peered inside, felt her breath catch, and quickly closed it.

Vomit rose in her throat. Her arms and legs trembled. She couldn't waste time standing there thinking about what she had just seen, though. The party was overflowing with gruesome props, but the contents of that freezer were definitely real. Lumikki glanced into the next freezer and sighed with relief. Nothing but a couple of bags of frozen peas at the bottom. Quickly, she switched off the freezer. It wouldn't help much, but at least she wouldn't lose all of her body heat instantly as the freezer strained to cool 120 pounds of teenager from 98.6 degrees to zero.

Lumikki saw the door move.

Climbing into the ice chest, she crouched in the most

comfortable position she could manage and then gently closed the lid just as the men stepped into the room.

The cold began nipping at her bare skin instantly. Even indoors, she couldn't seem to get away from freezing temperatures. This winter was cursed.

Terho Väisänen was impatient. He didn't have the energy for playing Boris Sokolov's games right now. All he wanted was time to polish his strategy for convincing Polar Bear that he deserved some proper severance pay. All the rumors said that no one could blackmail or threaten Polar Bear. No one had ever succeeded, though many had tried.

So he would have to negotiate.

"Where is Natalia?" Terho asked, still speaking English.

Boris Sokolov bared his teeth. The expression was probably meant as a smile.

"That's just what I wanted to show you," Sokolov replied. "Your Snow Queen is right here."

Väisänen watched in astonishment as Sokolov opened the lid of the nearest freezer.

Lumikki heard the retching sound Elisa's dad made, and she knew what he'd just seen. The image would probably be burned into her retinas for the rest of time. Material for future nightmares.

A young woman in a freezer, naked and dead.

Eyes open, face powder blue, with dark, dried blood on her lips. And a large hole in her stomach.

"What . . . what did you do to her?" Lumikki heard Elisa's father ask, his voice quavering.

"I'd think a cop would have seen a dead body before."

"But . . . why?"

"Are you really trying to tell me you didn't know? Natalia tried to run off with the money. Your money. Our money. We stopped her. You must have guessed when you got that bag full of bloody money."

"What money do you keep talking about?"

"Your compensation."

"Damn it, I keep telling you, the money never came."

"That's your problem, not ours. We made the delivery on February 28, as agreed. Three times a year, on the days you requested. But this time, we brought it to your house instead of hiding it in the woods. We thought you'd appreciate such good service."

"This is . . . nauseating."

"This is reality. We couldn't afford to let Natalia leave with the money. Losing thirty thousand euros might not be such a big deal, but the possibility of her informing on us was."

"I don't . . . I . . ." Elisa's father groped for the words. "I don't want to have anything to do with you or your men anymore. Ever. Is that clear? This wasn't supposed to happen. No one was supposed to die."

"Oh, but they have. First Natalia, and then Viivo."

"Viivo Tamm?"

"Polar Bear's men took him out. It was no big deal. Sometimes these things just happen. You should try to be professional about it too. There are always losses. Shipments disappear, money gets stolen, people die. It's all part of the business."

"Try to be professional? Professional? Fuck you. You killed a woman!"

Lumikki heard Terho Väisänen's voice break. He was on the verge of hysteria.

Lumikki could feel her fingers going numb. Her toes already had. Fortunately, she had plenty of oxygen in the freezer. So far.

"I offloaded an unreliable employee. And let me give you a little tip, Väisänen: Think twice before you start talking back to me. All I have to do is say the word and you'll be in there next to your whore. Hell, maybe I'll put you there myself."

Väisänen laughed, but there was an edge of desperation to it.

"But you need me. You've needed me for ten years now."

"Our arrangement has worked nicely. You've provided us with information, and we've revealed appropriate things to you in return. Our drug business has blossomed, and your narcotics squad's statistics have never looked better. It's a win-win. I'm the one you have to thank for your promotion. But you listen to me, Väisänen. I don't need you. You're like an ant to me. I can find a new informant anytime I want."

"That's good to hear, because I'm done."

"I decide when you're done."

"No, Boris, it isn't going down like that. I'm going to quit, and you can't do anything about it."

Lumikki listened to the silence between the men grow uncomfortable.

"Hmm," Sokolov finally said. "If you really did quit, how could I be sure you wouldn't squeal?"

"You'd just have to trust me."

"No. I'll tell you how. I could trust you because if you ever broke your word, you'd find that hot daughter of yours at home in your own freezer just like Natalia."

"You bastard."

Lumikki heard scuffling as Elisa's father attacked Sokolov. A moment later came a groan and then silence.

"I wasn't exaggerating when I said I would take you out myself if I needed to." Sokolov sounded out of breath.

"Okay. Okay. I get it. Just put that thing away. I'm sorry I lost it."

"Remember. Your daughter in a freezer. Cherish that image in your mind if you ever start feeling like you might do something stupid. I'll make it come true so fast your head will spin. And you know I'm a man of my word."

Then Lumikki heard the door open and the men exit.

Not a moment too soon. The cold had started to make her seriously numb, and the places her skin touched the freezer walls felt like they were getting frostbitten. Lumikki raised her arm to open the top of the chest.

Then the door opened again. Two sets of footsteps. An intense conversation in Finnish.

"I don't get how we can go through this much booze so fast. They're soaking it up like sponges."

"Better get used to it. This is just the beginning. Wait until you see what it's like after midnight."

Servers, Lumikki quickly deduced.

"What do we need most right now?"

"Bubbly. They always drink that most at the beginning. Then they start asking for white and red at about the same rate. Maybe more red when it's this cold out. After midnight, it's mostly harder stuff, whiskey and all that. A surprising amount of rum too. And vodka, of course. Some stick with the same thing the whole time, but most of them want variety."

Take the champagne and get out of here already, Lumikki hollered in her mind. *Go have your chat somewhere else.*

"Great. Someone stacked the red on top of the champagne again even though I clearly asked for bubbly on top, red on the bottom. Like I just said, they don't start drinking red wine until later."

"Big deal. Come on, let it go. Let's just move them out of the way."

"It is a big deal to me. This whole thing will blow up in our faces if people can't follow simple instructions. Listen, you have no idea what kind of chaos you're going to see here by the time this is over. It's pandemonium. We'll be carrying drinks with both arms, and it still won't be fast enough. Good luck finding some vintage cognac down here then with the system all messed up."

"Okay, I get it. Let's do this thing."

Lumikki silently thanked the second server for moving things along when she heard them start shifting crates. Bottles made muffled clinks.

"Not on the floor. They'll just be in the way there too. Let's put them on this freezer."

"Isn't there anything important in there? Something we might need soon? It would suck to have to keep lugging these crates all over the room. They weigh a ton."

"There's nothing in there but a few old bags of frozen vegetables. I just checked an hour ago."

"Maybe I should make sure."

Lumikki heard one of the servers grab the freezer lid handle.

Don't open it. Don't, don't, don't.

Then something heavy thudded down on top of the freezer.

"Hey, are you nuts? You could have crushed my fingers."

"Yeah, but I didn't. Are you going to help, or do I have to do everything myself?"

"Calm down."

Another thump on the lid. And a third. And a fourth. Four full crates of red wine.

"Now hop to it and grab that champagne already."

Clinking of bottles as each server lifted a crate. Steps receding toward the door.

"Hey, wait a sec," one of them said, turning back. Steps approached the freezer again. There was a click and the freezer compressor whirred into life.

"Someone must have turned it off by accident. You have to keep these things cold even if there are just a couple bags of peas in them. You never know when someone might want to freeze half a moose."

Steps toward the door again. The door opened and closed. Lumikki was alone in the storage room.

That is, if you didn't count the body of the woman named Natalia resting in the adjacent freezer.

Soon there might be two frozen corpses.

24

"COME ON! AT LEAST TRY. YOU HAVE TO SHOOT IT IN THE HEAD before it sees you. We keep losing points."

"Bite me! I'm doing my best. Stop bugging me. I can't concentrate."

"Now! Now! Shoot! Damn it, shoot!"

"Oh yeah! His ass is grass."

"Nice! That's what I'm talkin' about."

Elisa felt the headache pounding in her temples and the back of her head. She was sitting in front of her laptop, staring at a red dot that hadn't moved in hours. That was probably good. It meant that Lumikki had gotten inside the party. If she was stuck in the trunk of the car, she would have called or sent a text by now. Elisa wasn't willing to think about any of the other alternatives, like the driver or someone else finding Lumikki and making the trunk of the car her temporary coffin.

Fingertips gravitated toward her mouth, and Elisa tore at

her cuticles with her teeth. Her pink-and-black patterned gel nails had long since been ruined. What did it matter? She couldn't care less about stuff like fingernails and hair right now.

"I think this room could use some new paint. How about red? Oh, you think you can fight back, huh? Go ahead, make my day!"

That was it. Elisa had had enough. Marching over to the outlet, she pulled the PlayStation's cord out of the wall. Tuukka and Kasper's roars of protest were futile.

Go home and play if that's all you're capable of. Children.

"What the hell, Elisa? We almost had a high score," Kasper complained. "We were totally owning them."

"Can you two even imagine maybe concentrating on what's going on right now?" Elisa asked, pointing at her laptop.

"Come on, baby, chill. That picture hasn't changed for two hours. And it isn't going to change if everything goes like it should. We can't do anything to help Lumikki right now. Or do you think that if all three of us stare at the screen hard enough we can send her positive energy waves or some crap like that?"

Tuukka had walked up behind Elisa as he talked and now placed his hands on her shoulders. Elisa angrily shook them off. She couldn't stand Tuukka touching her now. Everything about him revolted her. She couldn't believe she had been in love with him once, that just a few days before she had thought they might end up together again once they'd both had time to prove their attractiveness with enough other people. That they were going to be the love story of the century.

If it weren't for Tuukka, Elisa wouldn't have to be staring at this scary red dot that represented Lumikki. She wouldn't have to be afraid for Lumikki or for her father. Tuukka had wanted to keep the money. Tuukka had come up with the brilliant idea of washing it at school. Fine, Elisa knew she was being unreasonable and that she couldn't really blame everything on this one boy being an ass, but directing her disgust at Tuukka helped her keep from thinking too hard about her father.

Her father. Daddy, as Elisa still thought of him. She'd always been a daddy's girl, especially since her mom had been traveling for work as long as she could remember. This was the daddy she invented silly games with. The daddy she dragged mattresses and blankets and pillows into the living room with to build giant forts. Sometimes they even slept in them. This was the daddy who made her pancakes shaped like teddy bears and sang bubblegum pop songs with her at the top of his lungs. The daddy who never got tired of her chatter or frustrated with her quirks. The daddy she cried to the first time a boy broke her heart. And barely a year had passed since their last Star Wars movie marathon, which always ended in an intergalactic popcorn war. Mom always just rolled her eyes.

The past few days had taken away the daddy Elisa thought she knew. In place of him, she now had this strange man who cheated on Mom with younger women and was mixed up in something dangerous and illegal. Elisa wished she could look her father straight in the eye and ask him, "Terho Väisänen, who are you, really?"

She was afraid for Lumikki, but was also afraid of what she might find out. The safest, most dependable thing in Elisa's life had been ripped away from her, and she wasn't sure whether she could deal with any more revelations. Not that she had a choice.

Tapping on his smartphone, Kasper suddenly looked up. "Uh-oh. I just realized something."

Elisa's pulse sped up. "What?"

"I doubt they let anyone keep their phones there. Polar Bear is supposed to be super strict about stuff like that," Kasper said.

"And you just thought of that?" Tuukka snapped. "How is she supposed to reach us, then?"

Elisa kept her cool.

"Lumikki can handle a problem like that. She'll come up with some way to let us know she's all right."

"You seem to trust her an awful lot," Tuukka said, looking at Elisa searchingly.

More than I trust you two, Elisa thought. Of course, she was grateful she didn't have to spend all night alone in her big house watching the red dot blinking on the screen. But she had decided that, once this was all over, she was going to put an end to her friendship with Tuukka and Kasper. They were never going to be a trio again.

Elisa's eye strayed back to the red dot showing the position of the Garmin locator unit. It was supposed to have helped her parents feel safe when she went jogging alone, but now Elisa only felt dread and guilt knowing where Lumikki was. What was Lumikki doing right now? What was she thinking? Elisa twirled a lock of blond hair and stuck the end in her mouth. Sucking on her hair had soothed her since she was little. She knew it annoyed Tuukka, but she didn't care.

"And if she doesn't tell us she's okay ..." Kasper left the sentence dangling unfinished in the air.

"Then we follow the original plan," Elisa said, trying to steady her voice.

"Where did you hide the GPS?" Tuukka asked.

"On her thigh," Elisa said. "On a garter strap."

"And what if someone notices it?" Kasper asked. "How do we know someone didn't rip it off and throw it in the trash and now Lumikki is dead and stuffed in some closet or dumped in the woods?"

Elisa stood up. She wanted to smack Kasper, or at the very least shove him.

"You shut up right now. Talking like that isn't going to help anything. Both of you shut up until you have something useful to say. Lumikki is there at the party and she's fine and everything is going the way it's supposed to. If she could hear us right now being all panicky, she'd probably laugh in our faces."

And with that, Elisa marched into the kitchen. She wanted something to calm her nerves. Her eyes landed on her mother's wine rack. Mom probably wouldn't notice one missing bottle. A couple of glasses of red wine would soften her thoughts and fears.

Elisa's fingers were already wistfully stroking the neck of a bottle, but she decided against it.

No, she had to keep herself sharp. She had to be ready if Lumikki needed help.

25

EACH CRATE CONTAINED SIXTEEN BOTTLES OF RED WINE. THERE were four crates. Each glass bottle contained 0.75 liters. Lumikki remembered reading somewhere that a glass wine bottle weighed one pound empty. Adding in the crates themselves, nearly 170 pounds of weight was sitting on top of the freezer. Not a pleasant thought.

Once, at the gym, Lumikki had managed to leg press 220 pounds. This wasn't a leg press machine, though. This was a freezer.

Lumikki kicked off her high heels. Then, bracing her lower back as well as she could against the bottom of the freezer, she thrust the soles of her feet against the underside of the lid. She pushed. Nothing.

Hypothermia: when a person's body temperature drops below ninety-five degrees Fahrenheit.

Symptoms: shivering, cold sensation, lack of coordination, twitching muscles.

As core temperature continues to fall, the feeling of cold disappears, muscle twitching stops, and mental acuity suffers. Respiratory and heart rates slow. When core temperature drops below eighty-six degrees, the risk of arrhythmia becomes significant.

At that point, the body's self-defense mechanisms begin moving warm blood closer to vital organs and cold blood to the extremities. The hands become disabled. Moving becomes difficult. Unnecessary movement of the extremities can cause cold blood to circulate, and when it reaches the heart, the resulting chilling of the heart muscle can cause ventricular fibrillation and even death.

Lumikki was no stranger to severe cold. That fall, after the breakup, she had started swimming regularly in the lake at the Winter Swimming Club's sauna. The cooler the water got, the better it felt. Diving into a hole in the frozen lake was one of the most amazing experiences of her life. Winter swimming was like a drug. With tiny ice crystals sloughing off her skin as she climbed out of the water, warmth would flood through her body, leaving her giddy from the endorphins singing in her veins. The feeling was amazing. You just wanted more and more and more.

Lumikki was the odd girl out at the sauna. Most of the regular visitors were old. Some of them wore knit hats in the steam of the 250-degree sauna, and all of them wore official Winter Swimming Club slippers. Lumikki hadn't bought a pair yet. The grandmas and grandpas generally called her "the girl." That suited her just fine. Lumikki had never seen anyone else under twenty at the sauna. Occasionally, groups of thirty-something men or women came for noisy bachelor or bachelorette parties.

Usually, though, the swimming hole, kept open year round by water left running from a hose, was quiet. Serious swimmers lowered themselves into the frigid water without any squeals or groans. They took a few strokes and then climbed out, standing on the patio of the sauna building for a while, letting their skin steam. Lumikki loved that moment. Seldom in her life had she experienced anything that could be called holy, but when she had visited the sauna one evening a week before Christmas with lanterns burning on the patio and stars shining in the sky and every cell in her body feeling completely awake after her swim, a strange gratitude had overwhelmed her, a mixture of longing, melancholy, and joy that contained a kernel of holiness. That moment was her Christmas mass, gazing at the stars and the spruce trees, heavy with snow, standing solemn and immovable.

But while the occasional dip in an icy lake was good for your health, lying in a freezer was not, under any circumstances. Thirty-two-degree water was different from a zero-degree coffin.

Right now, Lumikki wished she hadn't listened quite so carefully in health class. She forbade her brain from thinking about all the things lack of oxygen would do to her. She just had to focus on getting the lid open. It was all the same whether she moved her extremities too much or used up the oxygen in the freezer too quickly. Either she was going to get herself out or she was going to die.

Her legs were like frozen tree trunks.

Sucking in a deep breath, Lumikki tensed every muscle in her body and pushed, pushed, pushed.

The lid budged a little. Too little. Lumikki's strength faltered, and the lid clamped shut tight again.

Tears welled up in her eyes even though the last thing she wanted to do right now was cry. She felt so hopeless. Having everything end here was so stupid and pointless. She didn't want to die. Just when her time in Tampere had started making life feel worth living again.

Snow White in a glass coffin. Sleeping her eternal sleep.

No, she refused to let someone else write her story.

Lumikki thought of the girl she had been. That she was now. She had never given up. Not even in the darkest moments.

She adjusted her position a bit. Squeezing her eyes tight shut, she concentrated all her strength in her leg muscles. She hadn't done all those squats and lunges and leg presses and uphill sprints for nothing.

Muscles burning? Let them burn. Pain is just weakness leaving the body. And now for one more round. Sing along with the music if it helps!

Once more, Lumikki pushed and pushed and pushed. Her quadriceps shook. Pain burned in her thighs. Strange patterns flashed behind her shut eyelids.

She felt the lid lift. She didn't give up, showing her muscles no mercy. She heard the crates shifting. She heard them tip off and fall to the floor. She heard the glass breaking.

A ripple of tinkling glass like fairies ringing enchanted bells. The sweetest sound in the world.

Now she could stand up and push the lid open completely. She was trembling with cold and exhaustion. Red wine and glass shards covered the floor. Pulling her high heels back onto her feet, Lumikki climbed out of the freezer. High heels did have the advantage of only letting a very small portion of the sole touch the floor. Carefully placing her feet between the shards of glass, she cautiously moved toward the door.

Only now did she realize that she could have called for help. Maybe someone would have heard.

But that had never even crossed her mind. She had never called for help.

Boris Sokolov looked on as the other revelers began to relax more and more. He slowly sipped Jack Daniel's, his favorite whiskey. Polar Bear had remembered. Sokolov wasn't working now, so he could concentrate on whiskey and the nice view. Beautiful women—he was always happy to look at that. There was a touch of melancholy in his watching, though, since he knew he was old enough to be these women's father. One of them might keep him company for a night or two, but it wouldn't amount to anything serious. Sokolov's chance for a normal long-term relationship had long since passed. Dozens of lonely years with Jack Daniel's as his only real companion loomed ahead of him.

Polar Bear wanted to keep anything illegal out of these parties. A perfectly reasonable precaution. If the police did happen to raid one of them eventually, no one would get nailed for anything. This river of liquor was perfectly legit.

Sometimes Sokolov hated drugs. Yes, they gave him a

job and a comfortable life. A nice house without any neighbors too close. Influence. Women. And he wasn't too good to refuse a couple of lines of high-grade stuff, given the right opportunity, though he had never had any interest in shooting up.

But drugs also filled his life with constant stress. He had to make sure shipments arrived in Finland. He had to handle distribution, keep dealers in line, find new clients, and worry about old clients running their mouths. He always had too many irons in the fire. Balls were always falling on the floor.

Before, it was enough just to keep all the other Sergeis and Jorges and Mahmuds and Petters off his turf, but now he had to compete with the dot-coms too. Designer drugs had caught up with normal ones, and in some places galloped past. And to get those, all you had to do was sit down at your computer, go to some illegal website in the Netherlands, enter your order, and wait for the mailman to arrive. Fighting them was hopeless.

Polar Bear's idea that their target group was the rich, beautiful, and successful was great, but impossible to implement in practice. In order to make ends meet, they also had to deal to people who were so bottomed out that they could only pay in cash. Who had already sold their laptops or traded them for heroin. Whose bank transactions Social Services and their parole officers watched like hawks to make sure they were staying clean. Who didn't have the option of ordering online.

If the business hadn't been so dangerous, Sokolov wouldn't have needed to kill Natalia. In his own way, he had cared about her more than he'd ever admitted to himself. He'd even looked the other way when Natalia and Väisänen got together, even though it was a risk.

Boris had justified this leniency, telling himself that the relationship with Natalia was one more weapon in the arsenal of blackmail he might need to unleash on Väisänen at some point in the future. The stupid cop who swore he was done. He'd see about that. Boris was sure that Väisänen would come crawling back, begging to be let back in the game. And Boris would agree, of course, but with certain conditions. They had been letting their pet narcotics detective live a little too high on the hog. Väisänen had looked surprisingly sincere when he claimed not to have received the money. Maybe he was even telling the truth. Maybe someone had stolen the plastic bag from the yard that night. Boris didn't care, though. The money had been delivered to Väisänen, so Boris wasn't going to cry himself to sleep over it. The more important thing was that Väisänen seemed to be over it too. In the future, he wouldn't be getting nearly such hefty payoffs.

If Natalia had just stayed in line. She'd had a good, secure future ahead of her, the possibility of rising to be Boris's right hand. But she'd gotten restless and started to daydream. Boris had seen it happening, sensing the change in her face and tone of voice. He'd only needed to take one trip to Moscow and Natalia's brother had confessed his sister's entire plan.

Boris could have stopped Natalia simply by not leaving the money at his house. But he'd wanted to test her, to measure her loyalty. The gauge had swung to the minus side, even though he held out hope until the very end that she would come to her senses. Natalia hadn't left him any alternative to elimination. It was a shame. Boris had so hoped that Natalia would be the one person not to disappoint him.

The Jack Daniel's slid down his throat, smooth and warm. Still, Boris had to swallow a couple of extra times.

He would get rid of the body the next day.

Tonight was no time for dirty work.

26

MIDNIGHT WAS FAST APPROACHING. THE PARTY HAD TURNED louder and more restless. Music thundered. The drinks had morphed from wine to spirits. Women's makeup was beginning to smudge. Men were loosening their ties.

It wasn't quite time to cut loose completely, though, to throw out all sense of propriety and just drink as much free booze as possible, start picking fights, and disappear upstairs to "rest." The climax of the evening was yet to come.

The arrival of Polar Bear.

That was why Lumikki had stayed too. After escaping from the freezer, she had slipped into the ladies' room, removed her evening gown, and, standing over the toilet, drenched her arms and legs with warm water from the handheld bidet sprayer. Gradually, the feeling returned to her hands and feet. Then she dried herself off with hand towels, pulled her dress back on, and fixed her makeup, which had remained in remarkably good shape. Maybe Elisa really should consider a career in cosmetology. She'd succeeded in conjuring war paint for Lumikki that withstood not only eating and drinking but also freezing.

To the angry women lined up outside the bathroom door, she simply raised her eyebrows without saying a word.

Really, Lumikki could have left. She had accomplished her mission. She knew that Elisa's father was working with a drug dealer named Boris Sokolov. That he'd been giving Sokolov information and hiding information from the police in exchange for money. She also knew that the body of a woman named Natalia lay in a freezer in the basement and that Boris Sokolov had killed her. The information would most likely be enough to land Sokolov in jail. And Elisa's father too, of course, but that couldn't be helped.

But still, Lumikki stayed. Her curiosity would never be satisfied until she saw this mythical figure everyone spoke of in hushed tones and who had almost cost Lumikki her life. So she continued her tour of the fantasy rooms, which seemed to go on and on without end.

One room was completely pink. It probably would have been Elisa's favorite. Or maybe not, Lumikki realized after a few seconds. She felt a slight nausea when she noticed that, hidden among all the marshmallows, unicorns, rosebuds, and frilly pillows, there were various pink sex toys ranging from delicate whips to enormous dildos. Adult fairy tales for every taste, indeed. Lumikki removed herself quickly as an intertwined couple staggered into the room, looking like they might start using the goodies on offer at any moment.

The closer it got to midnight, the more electric the atmosphere became. Everyone was waiting. Everyone was keyed up. With ten seconds left, the countdown began. All the guests had gathered in the large ballroom on the second floor. People jostled and shoved.

Ten.

Glancing around, Lumikki saw Terho Väisänen nervously fidgeting with an empty glass.

Nine.

The music was turned down and then off.

Eight.

The lights dimmed. Only the stars projected on the ceiling remained.

Seven. Six. Five. Four. Three.

Lumikki almost burst out laughing, thinking of the absurdity of the situation. Here she was, a sensible teenage girl who just happened to walk into the school darkroom at the wrong moment.

Two.

People weren't yelling the numbers out anymore. They said them calmly, respectfully.

One.

Darkness swept over the room. Everyone fell silent. A muffled jingling like the sound of distant sleigh bells became audible. From the ceiling, flakes that looked like real snow began falling. When Lumikki touched one of them, it fell to dust.

Suddenly, powerful spotlights illuminated the center of the room.

Two women. Both in Snow Queen costumes. That name fit them a thousand times better than poor frozen Natalia.

Identical twins. They had somehow appeared out of thin air. Lumikki couldn't guess their age. They could just as easily have been twenty as fifty.

The ballroom erupted in ringing applause. The women waved majestically. Then Lumikki noticed that one of them was wearing a silver pendant in the shape of an ice crystal. The other woman's pendant was a silver bear.

Ice and a bear. Ice bear. Polar Bear. Not one person. Two. Who were still just one, singular.

The women waited for the crowd to calm down. Then they began to speak, switching back and forth so fluidly that Lumikki couldn't be sure which one was talking at any given moment.

"Winter is a time of enchantment. That's why I wanted the theme of this celebration to be fairy tales. Dreams, fantasies, and nightmares. These are the ingredients of fairy tales. You are all here because I wish to thank you. You have participated in creating a dream. A dream of a society more elegant, more efficient, more purposeful. For us, limits are made to be exceeded, rules to be changed, norms to be challenged. Celebrate! For one moment, forget the narrow boxes and expectations of the world outside. This is all for you. Life is for you."

There was nothing concrete, nothing to grab hold of in what the women said. They spoke perfect English without an accent. Even if Lumikki had been carrying a recorder, she wouldn't have gotten anything incriminating. What were these women involved in? What dirt did they have on all these party guests? How many of their businesses were criminal?

Looking over the adoring crowd, Lumikki understood that she'd probably never know. Polar Bear's real activities were like the fake snow falling from the ceiling. If you tried to grab hold of them, they disintegrated and disappeared.

She would never have a chance against these people. And the twins themselves might simply be a facade. No one would catch them. No one could do anything to them.

What Lumikki could do, though, was put Boris Sokolov behind bars. The events that began with the bloody cash in the darkroom could come full circle. That would be enough.

Now she wanted to go home.

27

"I DON'T NEED A LOOKING GLASS TO TELL ME YOU'RE THE FAIR-est woman at this party."

Hot breath wafted against Lumikki's ear, and firm hands grabbed at her waist. Lumikki swore to herself. Her tormenter had found her again and succeeded in capturing her in a surprisingly tight grip just as she was intending to leave. She could smell from his breath that he had imbibed more than a few rounds of cognac. Lumikki could tell from his grip that she had no hope of wriggling free. It would only attract unwanted attention if she tried.

"I was starting to worry that you'd disappeared. That would be unacceptable. We were interrupted so regrettably," the man whispered, pressing his broad carcass against Lumikki's back.

At least two hundred pounds, Lumikki guessed. Might be surprisingly strong when provoked. Time for a different tactic now.

"You haven't gone cold on me already, have you?"

Fortunately not, Lumikki thought.

Turning around, she looked the man in the face. His eyes were bloodshot. He had left his tuxedo jacket somewhere. Large, dark patches ran outward from his armpits across his powder-blue shirt. His tie was a little loose. With a gesture full of false self-assurance, she took hold of the man's tie, drew his ear to her mouth, and whispered, "Let's go upstairs and see if this story has a happily ever after."

Then she nibbled at his earlobe, forcing down her disgust. She could play this role too.

A satisfied blush spread across the man's face, and he licked his lips.

"What are we waiting for?" he asked.

As she climbed the stairs, Lumikki could feel the man's constant gaze on her back. Trying to escape would be pointless. Her legs were trembling a bit, but she forced herself to swing her hips invitingly as she walked. What would it be like to ascend these stairs ahead of someone she really wanted to be with, to pull a door shut behind them and lock the rest of the world outside? The smell of sunscreen and warm skin. Laughing as she ran up the wooden steps of the boat dock at the cabin. Footsteps following steadily. Tingling in anticipation as she listened to them come.

Reminiscing was pointless. Last summer was an eternity ago. Now was now, and she should do this.

Lumikki led the man to a free room, in the middle of which was a large wrought-iron bed. She shoved him down on the mattress. It was important to be as self-assured and bold as possible.

"I knew you were a wildcat! But that's okay, I'll tame you," he said, beginning to pull his trousers off while still lying on the bed. Lumikki shut the door and turned the key in the lock with a click. Then she sashayed toward the man, who tried to grope her with his sweaty hands.

"Tsk-tsk, kitty wants to toy with you first, remember," Lumikki said, pushing him down.

To Lumikki's relief, his drunken eyes lit up. He was at her mercy, at least for the moment. Lumikki climbed onto the bed and straddled her victim, who immediately began stroking her thighs hungrily.

"What's this . . . ?" the man asked, his forehead wrinkling in confusion as he found the GPS tracker.

Oh shit. Swiftly, Lumikki grabbed the man's hands and forcefully pulled them up toward the headboard.

"Now be a good boy," she whispered, holding the man's wrists with her left hand while she dug something fluffy and pink out of her purse with her right.

"Oh, so you're into bondage?" the man said with a grin.

Lumikki snapped the handcuffs shut around his wrists and fastened them to the iron bed frame.

"Not really," she replied, and stood up. "But I hope you are."

It took the man a few seconds to realize that Lumikki had no intention of returning to the bed. When it finally dawned on his cognac-clouded brain and an enraged roar erupted from his lips, it was already too late. Lumikki had locked the door from the outside.

Then she walked to the window at the end of the hall. Opening it, she tossed the room key and the key to the handcuffs out into the snow, where they disappeared instantly. One less obstacle to her getting home.

Terho Väisänen stared out a large window into the darkness.

He'd given up, realizing there was no way he could convince Polar Bear that she should pay him off and let him go. Or they. How was he supposed to address them? He had tried to talk to one of the women's bodyguards and request a meeting. His request was denied. When he explained that he had received a special invitation to meet Polar Bear, the bodyguard coldly informed him that his invitation meant nothing. He shouldn't waste his time imagining that Polar Bear would be interested in a nobody like him.

And when he looked around at the other guests, he understood that the bodyguard was right. He was little more than a gnat to Polar Bear. Even Boris Sokolov was only a gnat, or at most a fly. They were ludicrously small players in some larger game.

All Terho could do was retreat with his tail between his legs. Go home, hug his daughter, and write his wife an email telling her that he missed her. Think about how to make ends meet without his most important source of income. The situation wasn't hopeless. Yes, he had debt, but he also had a job. And so did his wife. They could cut back on their expenses. He would have to stop gambling, of course, but that had been part of his plan for a while now. He wouldn't need money to help Natalia anymore, since there was no Natalia. Terho's hands began to shake, and he felt sick to his stomach just thinking about that. He had to put it out of his head. He couldn't let that pain take over now. He had to stay rational. He had to think practically. His daughter didn't always need to have the most expensive everything. Slowing down, simplifying their life, and spending more time together would do the whole family good. Live a normal life like everybody else.

Normal people's lives didn't include passing information to crime bosses about when and where the police would be conducting their next raid, what dealers were informants, what trucks would be stopped at the border, or what campaigns were in the works to weed out drug trafficking. Normal people's lives also didn't include being tipped off about drug stashes or small-time crooks that Sokolov's gang wanted to get rid of for some reason. Over the years, Terho had solved an embarrassing number of crimes with Sokolov's help. He had told himself that they both benefited from the agreement.

Sokolov wanted a monopoly on the Tampere drug trade, and Terho wanted to lock up the dangerous dealers who sold contaminated mixtures and outright poison in place of genuine product and were responsible for most of the drug deaths.

He had assuaged his conscience by telling himself that Sokolov mostly sold to people who had their habits under control and weren't going to end up in the ER with overdoses. Recreational users. But he had known for a long time that that was only part of the truth. Sokolov was also perfectly happy to take money from people who would have been better off buying bread and milk for their children. Terho had just wanted to bury his head in the sand.

He wanted to bury his head in the sand now too. Suddenly, he was painfully tired. He needed to get out of there.

Just then, Terho noticed the same young woman whose dress had caught his attention earlier. This time, he also noticed her white beaded handbag. Generally, he didn't know the first thing about women's purses, but this particular one he happened to know a lot about. A Hermès original, it cost hundreds of euros. He knew because he had bought exactly the same bag for Elisa as a birthday present since she had been begging for it for so long.

A similar evening gown could be a coincidence.

A similar purse could be a coincidence.

But both of them together on the same woman couldn't be.

With a few steps, Terho strode over to the woman, took her firmly by the arm, and demanded an explanation.

Boris Sokolov's interest perked up when he saw Terho Väisänen arguing with a young woman. Moving closer, he grasped enough of Väisänen's Finnish to understand that he was claiming to have bought the woman's handbag and dress. And shoes.

Boris snorted. Apparently, Väisänen had been spending his money on women besides Natalia. That would have to end now too. He was already turning back the way he had come when he caught the word *tytär. Daughter.*

That stopped Boris in his tracks. His brain raced a million miles an hour. If the girl in the red dress was Terho Väisänen's daughter, it was clear she knew too much. She knew who had chased her in the woods. She might even know about Natalia. And the money. Why else would she be here at the party?

He'd better go talk to her and make sure she knew to keep her mouth shut just like her father.

Lumikki tried to wrench her arm free of Elisa's father's grasp, but as a police officer, he was clearly used to dealing with uncooperative people. His grip was like iron.

"Answer me! Why do you have Elisa's purse?"

Lumikki could see Boris Sokolov approaching. Something in his eyes scared her.

Väisänen was oppressively close.

He sniffed the air. "You're even wearing her perfume!" he snapped.

Sokolov was only three steps away.

Lumikki had to get away.

Forcefully, she shoved Elisa's handbag against her father's chest.

"Fine, take it. Unfortunately, I can't return the perfume."

Väisänen was thrown off guard enough that his grip loosened ever so slightly. It was enough. Lumikki tore herself away and rushed toward the stairs. She heard Sokolov coming after her, bellowing something in Russian.

At the stairs, she ran into a server dressed as Alice in Wonderland and carrying some sort of dairy-based drinks. Maybe white Russians. Silently apologizing, Lumikki knocked the serving tray out of the woman's hands. Liquid and shards of glass spread across the stairs. She heard Sokolov slip and swear.

That bought Lumikki a few precious seconds. Snatching her high heels off her feet, she burst through the crowd, clutching the shoes in her hands. To the front door and out into the night. She continued running along the candlelit path.

Fire walk with me. This whole thing was starting to feel more and more like something from *Twin Peaks.* All that was missing was the dwarf.

Sokolov yelled to the guards on the stairs. "Stop her!"

The men turned and blocked her way, two refrigerators she didn't stand a chance of getting past.

Lumikki swerved and changed direction. Sokolov followed. A high wall surrounded the building on every side. Lumikki ran to the farthest corner. It was dark. The snow stung the soles of her feet, which were covered only with thin pantyhose.

Lumikki quickly scanned the wall with her hand. There was nothing to grip. Even a monkey wouldn't have been able to climb it. But then she found a small hole. Stabbing the point of one of her heels deep into the hole, she climbed up and stood on the shoe. She nearly lost her balance. Sokolov was almost to the wall.

Driving the other shoe into the wall heel first, she took another big step up. Sokolov seized the hem of her dress.

The hem ripped.

The shoe broke.

The shoe fell into the snow, leaving only the thin heel stuck in the wall. Lumikki's feet flailed in the air without any support. However, her fingers clung to the top of the wall, and she just managed to pull herself up as Sokolov's hand grazed her foot.

Lumikki dropped down on the other side, landing in a

soft snowdrift. Instead of trying to get over the wall himself, Sokolov took off running, presumably toward the gate. Lumikki ran through the snow, which came up to her calves. The hem of her evening gown was ripped on one side, revealing her entire thigh.

Good, Lumikki thought as she ran. Otherwise, moving would be harder.

Running in the snow was difficult, and the cold bit with razor teeth. The forest was as dark as blackness itself.

Sokolov was falling farther and farther behind, though. Lumikki sped up. This was the third time in four days that someone had chased her and she'd had to run away through the snow and cold.

Three tries. In fairy tales, the heroes always got three tries. The first two failed, but the third succeeded. Did that mean that she would get away once and for all? Or that her pursuers would finally catch her?

Third time's the charm. Three strikes and you're out. Which one was this?

Suddenly, Lumikki felt something painfully scratch her bare thigh. She ignored it. She just ran and waded and struggled on. Finally, the sounds of pursuit faded.

Lumikki brushed her thigh with her fingers, which came back with something warm and wet. Blood. Sokolov had shot her in the thigh, but luckily, the bullet had only grazed her. Blood was flowing heavily, though.

Lumikki didn't want to think about it.

She just ran. The forest embraced her like dark water.

But now the poor child was all alone in the great forest. So afraid was she that, seeing all the leaves on the trees, she knew not whither to turn for help. Then she began to run and ran over the sharp rocks and through the thorns, and wild beasts jumped at her but passed by, doing her no harm. On she ran as long as her legs would carry her, and night began to fall.

28

ONCE UPON A TIME, THERE WAS A GIRL WHO RAN SO FAR HER legs couldn't carry her anymore. And then she continued to run, in her mind, in her dreams. Her slender, strong, agile legs dashed over the drifts, leaving nary a print in the soft white snow. She fled as those flee who know they are free, who know that no one will catch them.

Lumikki teetered on the border between consciousness and oblivion.

She was no longer cold. She was warm. At some level, she knew that was a bad thing, but she didn't care anymore. She lay on her back in the snow.

She thought of the blood trickling from her thigh into the snow. She imagined how the red would form beautiful spirals against the white, painting a gorgeous pattern that would spread a few feet, a few more, out across the entire forest.

She saw herself from above as if she were floating thirty feet in the air. Black hair arrayed against the snow like a halo. An evening gown that, even torn, glowed as though spun from red rubies. Twisting patterns that extended, growing organically.

Beautiful. Not ugly.

Ugly. Fat. Too skinny. Weird teeth. Annoying voice. Greasy hair. Dirty shoes. Hairy arms. Stupid. Idiot. Weirdo. Bitch. Whore.

Where did you get those clothes? Out of the trash?

Your parents are probably ashamed to go out in public with you.

If I looked like that, I'd never leave home.

You must be adopted.

No one will ever want to kiss you.

No one could love somebody like you.

Why are you crying? If it hurts, say so. Oh, it hurts? Shut up or I'll give you a real reason to cry.

You're so ugly, you actually look better with bruises.

Words, words, words, words, words, words, words, words. Phrases, sentences, questions, shouts. Pinching, scratching, hitting, dragging, pulling, shoving, kicking.

You aren't those words. You aren't the shouts and names. You aren't the awful things spat at you like flavorless gum. You aren't the punches or the bruises they cause. You aren't the blood running from your nose. You aren't under their control. You are not theirs.

Inside you is always the part of you that no one can touch.

You are you. You are your own, and inside you is the universe. You can be whatever you want. You can be anyone.

Don't be afraid. You don't have to be afraid anymore.

"I don't have to be afraid anymore," Lumikki whispered quietly to herself.

Steam rose from her mouth.

She still remembered their faces. Their girlish voices and laughs that echoed, echoed, echoed down the halls of the school even after the day had ended and the building was silent.

She remembered the smells especially. In the early years, it was the cloying imitation aromas of scented erasers. Then sweets eaten secretly at recess, raspberry hard candies and licorice together. A breath in her face, sweet and salty inter-mixed. Toffee, mango, and peppermint lip gloss. Body Shop vanilla perfume, the first one their mothers would let them wear at school. Then later, the real perfumes that changed with the day, the mood, the clothes, and the trends. Escada's scent of the season.

She learned to recognize them quickly and precisely, smelling them from a distance so she could tell when they would turn the corner. Sometimes it helped. Sometimes she had time to hide. But usually it didn't. Then she learned how nauseating perfume can really smell when its stench mixes with sweat, or how an unwashed urinal in the boys' bathroom stinks when your head is shoved in it and you're ordered to lick the cold, hard porcelain.

She remembered their names. She would always remember their names.

Anna-Sofia and Vanessa.

It had lasted from first grade to the middle of ninth. Every year, the hands were stronger, the words crueler, the blows more painful. Lumikki didn't know why the girls had chosen her. Maybe she'd smiled the wrong way or not smiled at all. Maybe she'd used the wrong tone of voice at the wrong time. It didn't matter. She'd learned quickly that she would never be able to change herself or her behavior enough to make Anna-Sofia and Vanessa leave her in peace.

Lumikki had never told anyone. She'd never even considered it an option. Silence had been the general rule at home. Don't ask, don't tell. Everything was good if nothing bad was said out loud. The bruises, the scrapes, the sprained wrists, the ripped clothing. Everything could be explained if an explanation was necessary. School had been a battlefield, and Lumikki could never be sure who was a friend and who was an enemy. Her strategies had required careful thought. Try to minimize casualties. Telling the teachers would just have made the situation worse. She had to assume they wouldn't believe her. Anna-Sofia and Vanessa knew how to playact in front of the adults. Their smiles were angelic and innocent.

Violence, torture, and subjugation. Lumikki refused to think of what she experienced as bullying because that sounded like something minor, transitory, and simple. Just a little fun. Just a little kidding. Just a little shoving. Oh, she fell on her own. We were only joking.

In the eighth grade, Lumikki secretly started running and lifting weights. She had decided to be in the best physical condition she could so she could run away. That had worked a little better every time, but it hadn't made the nightmare end.

Then once, on a late, wintry afternoon when the sun had

already disappeared below the horizon and the schoolyard was empty, Lumikki hid behind the compost bin until she was sure Vanessa and Anna-Sofia had left. She had endured the stench of banana peels and pea soup leftovers that filled the frozen air, radiating with the heat of the decomposition process. She waited until everything was silent. A blue dusk fell over the schoolyard. Peace.

Lumikki left her hiding place. She moved noiselessly. She melted into the gray shadows, little more than a breath of wind on the trampled snow. She heard the sounds of cars from blocks away. She heard dogs barking in a distant park. She heard snow sliding off the school roof. But she heard Vanessa and Anna-Sofia's footsteps too late. Too late, she dashed off on legs newly filled with explosive power. It just wasn't enough. The girls drove her into the back corner of the yard, where high brick walls rose up. Running toward the wall, Lumikki pulled off her mittens and shoved them in her pockets. She grabbed the wall's rough bricks with her fingers and tried to climb. Her feet couldn't find any purchase. Her fingers froze in the cold air and wouldn't hold on. She was trapped.

Lumikki turned, pressing her back against the brick wall and preparing to receive their blows. She had learned how to take a hit. She already knew how best to shield herself. She knew when to breathe in and when to breathe out, when to tense her muscles and when to relax. She just hoped the beating wouldn't last very long today. She was cold and needed to pee. She wanted to go home. She wanted to eat her dad's slightly burned fish sticks and do her homework and not think anything.

Anna-Sofia and Vanessa approached. They didn't say

anything. Silence was worse than insults and threats, condensing into an anticipation that brought the taste of bile to Lumikki's mouth. The girls crept toward her softly like wolves. Lumikki would have preferred to meet hungry, angry wolves than this pair, whose hair shone in the dusk, their lips sparkling red. These were much more dangerous creatures, with ice in place of warm blood pumping through their hearts.

Slowly, Lumikki counted down from ten, waiting for the first breach of her physical borders. She didn't know whether it would be a light shove on the shoulder, a swift kick in the stomach, or a glop of peppermint spit in her face.

Ten, nine, eight, seven . . .

Suddenly, Lumikki felt something hot and red growing inside. It was strange. It didn't feel like it was coming from her. Anger. Rage. A blinding desire not to be afraid. The numbers disappeared, thought disappeared, time and place disappeared. Afterward, she could never say what had happened. A piece of her memory was missing. A gaping hole in the time line.

She was sitting on Anna-Sofia in the snow, punching her in the face with all her might. On her knuckles was something warm and dark. Dimly, she understood that it was blood from Anna-Sofia's nose. She more sensed than felt that Vanessa was trying to tear her off. Lumikki's elbow made contact with Vanessa's stomach, and the girl let go.

Lumikki didn't know how long she had been pummeling Anna-Sofia. She was watching herself from somewhere far away. A girl with tears and snot running uncontrollably down her cheeks and jaw. Whose arms rose and fell less powerfully with every stroke. Was that really her? Wasn't it supposed to be the other way around? Anna-Sofia whimpering and protecting her face, Vanessa holding her stomach and screaming for Lumikki to stop. Wasn't that backward? Then Lumikki burst back into her own body, feeling Anna-Sofia's soft, submissive form under her, and the rage was gone.

She stood. Her legs trembled. Her hands hung limp. The cold nipped at her fingers. She wiped her wet face. Anna-Sofia sat up, hunched over, and Vanessa knelt next to her. They did not look Lumikki in the eye. Lumikki did not look them in the eye. No one said anything. Silence spoke louder than words.

With shaking, exhausted legs, Lumikki set off toward home. She was not afraid that the girls would follow her and try to get revenge. She was not afraid of anything. She did not feel anything. She did not think anything. Halfway home, she stopped on the side of the road and vomited. The pea soup looked surprisingly similar to how it had before being eaten.

At home, she slipped straight into the bathroom before her parents could see. The girl who looked back from the mirror was a stranger. On her cheeks were streaks of blood. In wonder, Lumikki raised her hands and touched them. The girl in the mirror did the same. The blood was not hers. It was Anna-Sofia's blood. Lumikki washed her face once, twice, three times, four times with water as hot as she could stand. She scrubbed her hands with soap until they stung.

After finally getting in bed that night, she drifted off immediately and slept long into the morning without dreaming. When a beep from her cell phone woke her up, she felt worse than she ever had before. Worse than the mornings after she'd been beaten black-and-blue.

Lumikki was sure things wouldn't end there. Anna-Sofia

and Vanessa would never let it go. She would be punished one way or another, officially or not. They would never give up on revenge.

One day passed, then two, three, a week, a month. Nothing happened. Anna-Sofia and Vanessa simply left her alone. Yes, she was still isolated from the rest of her class and no one spoke to her voluntarily, but there were no more beatings. Or names. Or text messages threatening to kill her.

Everything just stopped.

Gradually, Lumikki began to trust it. She breathed more easily. Spring came, bringing with it more light and fewer school days. As she listened to the others singing *"Den blomstertid nu kommer,"* the hymn they always sang at every graduation, Lumikki felt something heavy and black release its grip on her. With her ninth-grade diploma in hand, she walked out into the streaming sunlight, summer, and freedom.

The snow shone yellow. Then orange. Then a moment later, green. Lumikki saw the lights and heard a pop. Golden stars fell from the sky. Then enormous roses burst into life, their petals opening, melting, and vanishing. A unicorn struggled toward the moon. The planets danced. Fireworks.

In honor of Polar Bear.

It was probably almost twelve-thirty.

Lumikki thought of the small tracker strapped to her thigh. She considered the instructions she had given Elisa to call the police in case she didn't return from the party or report back by midnight.

She had to leave the party before the clock struck twelve.

But wasn't that a different story? Cinderella?

The crackling continued. Lumikki floated on multi-colored waves. She felt fine. Just tired.

"Every evening when the lamp turns out and real night arrives."

Wasn't that how the lullaby went?

Wasn't that how the blue dream began?

Blue, blue, sparkling blue.

For a moment, Lumikki thought the fireworks were still going. Then she realized that she wasn't hearing explosions anymore. A wailing started.

A white wall. A sterile smell. Bright lights.

Sickening, pulsating pain somewhere far away. Lumikki couldn't think about it. The taste of antibiotics in her mouth.

Drip, drip, drip. Something was flowing into her. She was attached to something. She vaguely remembered that there were names for all these things surrounding her. She didn't have the strength to think of them, though.

Figures moving in front of the lights.

Familiar faces.

Mom. Dad.

Sounds from far away, behind glass, above the surface of the water, on the other side of a wall.

"The doctor said she's turned a corner. Don't cry, darling. *Älskling.* She'll be all right. She's a fighter."

"I just can't stop thinking. I don't think I could survive if we lost her too."

"We won't. Hush. Hush."

Too? Who had Mom and Dad lost? Lumikki wanted to

ask, but she couldn't form the words. Opening her mouth would have taken an overwhelming effort. She just wanted to sleep. She would have to remember to ask later. Sometime later. After she had slept for a hundred years.

But wasn't that a different story? Sleeping Beauty?

Lumikki felt herself sinking into the bed, into its softness, slipping through the mattress as if through layers of cloud, and flying.

EPILOGUE

FOUR MONTHS LATER

On the card was a black-and-white photograph of a muscular naked man holding a kitten in a strategic location. Lumikki didn't even need to turn the card over to guess who it was from.

> *Hey, girl!*
> *Everything's okay here. Mom isn't as nervous as before, and I'm sleeping through the night without waking up all the time, and I don't even look behind myself all the time when I'm walking down the street now. It's been good for me to have some free time away from everything. I'm applying for cosmetology school here. If I get in, I start in the fall. I'm pretty sure that's going to be my thing.*
> *Jenna*

*PS I'm already used to my new name. I don't
turn around anymore when someone shouts my old
name on the street or anything.*

*PPS I haven't been to see Dad. Maybe someday.
I still can't deal. I'm sure you understand. I can't
even write anything about it without starting to
cry.*

*PPPS I knitted you some gloves. They'll come in
the mail later. Sorry it took a while. It's too late
for you to need them now, but you'll have them
next fall.*

Lumikki smiled. She glanced out the window. Elisa, or,
well, Jenna now, was right. It was already the end of June and
bewilderingly hot. Everything was blooming and radiant.

It was good to hear she was doing well. Her dad had gone
to jail, along with Boris Sokolov. They'd been prosecuted with
unusual speed. The police department had been anxious to
get it over with as fast as possible so they could start cleaning
up their image. Both had received long sentences. Sokolov's
Estonian sidekick Linnart Kask had also been sent to prison.
Elisa and her mother had moved to another part of the coun-
try and changed their names. That was probably smart under
the circumstances. Elisa had sworn up and down to Child
Protective Services that she was done with drugs. Lumikki
believed her. Elisa and her mom would have to find a totally
new way to live their lives and be a family. That wasn't necessarily all bad.

Lumikki's left hand gravitated to the short-cropped hair at the back of her neck. She still wasn't used to such a short hairdo, although it did feel liberating. Once her roots had become obvious under her dyed black bob, she made the decision. A never-ending spiral of hair dyeing wasn't appealing, and she hated the way the combination of fair skin and dark hair drew attention to her name. So, super short hair and her natural color it was. She also liked how simple the style was.

The truth was, it felt safer to see a completely different girl staring back from the mirror than the one who had attended Polar Bear's party. Not that she was actually afraid of anyone from the party recognizing her on the street. People were surprisingly blind when visual images were removed from their original contexts. Since no one could imagine that a girl with no makeup, traipsing down the street in old combat boots and a green army jacket, could ever have been at a high-class party, the conclusion was obvious: She hadn't been there. The human mind was just that simple. Stupid, really, but so lucky for her.

Over the past two months, Elisa/Jenna had sent Lumikki cards a few times. Lumikki kept them under the false bottom of the top drawer of the dresser in her old room.

Yes, she was living at home again. In Riihimäki, that is, in the house where she grew up. After the events of the winter, the police had interrogated her first, and then her parents had. She had told both only the bare minimum. Her parents had insisted that she move back home "at least for the time being." Lumikki tolerated it even though her old room was so full of the past and felt so small. She commuted back to school in

Tampere by train, even though that meant waking up at an inhuman hour.

For the time being.

Lumikki hoped she'd be able to convince her parents over the summer that it was safe for her to live alone in Tampere again.

No one looked at her strangely at school because no one knew. Kasper and Tuukka had been expelled when the news about their drug use and the school break-in had come out. Everything had been handled as quietly as possible. There were rumors around school, of course, but no one knew to connect Lumikki to them. Some of the rumors were pretty wild, but none of them even approached the insanity of the truth.

Terho Väisänen was in prison. Boris Sokolov was in prison. Polar Bear was not. Were not.

Lumikki had kept her mouth shut tight about them in her interviews. She knew that if she talked, she'd only be hurting herself. She didn't have any proof that the twins were involved in anything illegal. She didn't actually know anything about them.

And the police didn't ask. The party venue had been in Boris Sokolov's name, and everything else was routed through him too. Officially, there was no Polar Bear. No one had ever seen or heard of him, her, or them.

Lumikki idly stroked the edge of the postcard. Strange that Elisa preferred to send cards rather than writing emails. That was another flaw in her shiny image, an aberration that, to her own surprise, made Lumikki really value the girl's friendship. She had thought of Elisa when painting a tiny pink rose in the bottom corner of her *Girlfriends* painting. You wouldn't even notice it unless you looked closely.

She put the card with the others. Under the dresser drawer, there was also an envelope she'd received immediately after getting home from the hospital. Inside were two five-hundred-euro bills. A thousand euros. It was such a small part of thirty thousand that no one would miss it. She didn't know whether Elisa, Tuukka, and Kasper had hidden any more. She didn't want to know.

A thousand euros was enough of a secret.

Lumikki was used to having secrets. She had always had them, sometimes big, sometimes small. Closing the dresser drawer, she imagined that she was also putting away the other secrets she didn't have the evidence to prove.

Polar Bear and the fact that she'd met them.

Anna-Sofia and Vanessa and what they had done to her during elementary and middle school.

The important person Mom and Dad had lost, but who she hadn't been able to work up the courage to ask about. In a house furnished with taboos, you didn't just start redecorating like it was nothing.

And one more secret. The one whose picture Lumikki was holding now. Of course, a photograph was physical evidence that the person in it was real, but nothing proved that Lumikki had loved him. That he had loved Lumikki. If he had. Lumikki wanted to believe he had.

She stroked the picture carefully with her thumb. Short, light brown hair that shifted from wheat to hazel. A cheek, a shoulder, an arm. Captivated once again by those eyes so blue they made you think of a purebred husky. Some people thought those eyes were piercing, scornful. Lumikki saw deeper. She saw the warmth, the uncertainty, the joy, the light.

Longing clenched her stomach with astonishing strength. Lumikki thought it had eased by now. She was as wrong as wrong can be.

The name was already tingling on her lips. The name she had whispered and cried aloud. She wasn't over it yet. She wasn't ready to move on. Not now, maybe not ever.

Lumikki locked the drawer, even though she knew it was safe. She held the small, tarnished key in her hand. It gleamed, but dimly. It was plain and inconspicuous.

Once upon a time, there was a little key that could fit in any lock.

Fairy tales don't begin that way. That's how other, brighter stories begin.

ABOUT THE AUTHOR

Salla Simukka's As Red as Blood trilogy is an international bestseller, having sold more than one million copies worldwide in fifty-two territories and as a Hollywood film. Inspiration for her runaway hit started in a German bookstore. While browsing the children's section, she was struck by the fables displayed next to the crime section. Suddenly, she had three titles in her head (*As Red as Blood, As White as Snow, As Black as Ebony*) and a trilogy that demanded to be written.

As Red as Blood is Simukka's first work to publish in the United States, but she has already written several novels and a collection of short stories. She has also translated adult fiction, children's books, and plays, and worked as a TV screenwriter before turning her attention to writing full time. Simukka lives in Tampere, Finland.

ABOUT THE TRANSLATOR

Owen F. Witesman is a professional literary translator with a master's in Finnish and Estonian area studies from Indiana University. He has translated more than thirty Finnish books into English, including novels, children's books, poetry, plays, graphic novels, and nonfiction. His recent translations include the novels *My First Murder, Her Enemy, Copper Heart, Snow Woman, Death Spiral,* and *Fatal Headwind* from the Maria Kallio series by Leena Lehtolainen; the satire *The Human Part* by Kari Hotakainen; the thrillers *Cold Courage* and *Black Noise* by Pekka Hiltunen; Risto Isomäki's ecothriller *Lithium-6*; and the nonfiction opus *The Mapmakers' World* by Marjo Nurminen. He currently resides in Springville, Utah, with his wife and three daughters, one son, two dogs, a cat, and thirty-odd fruit trees.